YOLI'S FAVORITE THINGS

YOLI'S FAVORITE THINGS

PATRICIA SANTANA

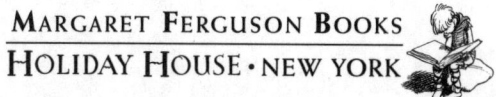

Margaret Ferguson Books
Holiday House · New York

Margaret Ferguson Books
An imprint of Holiday House Publishing, Inc.

Copyright © 2025 by Patricia Santana
All Rights Reserved
HOLIDAY HOUSE is registered in the U.S. Patent and Trademark Office.
Printed and bound in July 2025 at Sheridan, Chelsea, MI, USA.
www.holidayhouse.com
First Edition
1 3 5 7 9 10 8 6 4 2

Library of Congress Cataloging-in-Publication Data is available.

ISBN: 978-0-8234-5948-3 (hardcover)

EU Authorized Representative: HackettFlynn Ltd, 36 Cloch Choirneal,
Balrothery, Co. Dublin, K32 C942, Ireland. EU@walkerpublishinggroup.com

For Judy Violet

YOLI'S FAVORITE THINGS

ONE

Every Friday, Miss Toscano ended class with parting words of wisdom. "Class," she'd announced today in the low tone of voice she used when she was about to say something of great import. "In life, it is best to concentrate on the positive. Always live in the positive."

I was dying to raise my hand and ask her what we were supposed to do with the *other* thoughts, the ones that brought on worries and fears. The ones that grabbed hold of my heart and squeezed every time I heard the word *war* or *Vietnam*.

Instead, I'd nodded and glanced at the other sixth graders, and then at my best friend, Lydia, who looked at me and shrugged. Did she understand what our teacher meant? Did I?

Later that afternoon I was thinking about Miss Toscano's words as I sat with my diary on the three rickety wooden steps near the top of the canyon. It looked like somebody had a plan for these steps and then decided to abandon the project. But I made good use of them, my little perch with an unobstructed view of the canyon. Perfect breezy, sunny weather for the end of March. The ravine below held a jungle of tangled brambles and a swath of yellow blooms, punctuated with eucalyptus and pepper trees, and just beyond that was Interstate 5. Staring at the cars zooming past on the freeway, I was trying to concentrate on the fun parts of my favorite movie, *The Sound of Music*—the grand estate in the Austrian countryside, the cheery songs, the dreamy romance, the big family like ours—and not on the things in my life that were troubling me.

It was hard for me to explain my fascination with the movie—what Lydia called my *utterly obsessive enthrallment*—but it was so. My two older sisters, Carolina and Ana, had taken me to see it two years ago for my tenth birthday. With her newly issued driver's license, Carolina was quick to volunteer her services as the designated chauffeur to anywhere and everywhere.

As we climbed into the Rambler, my favorite brother, Chuy, came out of the house. "Hold on," he called to us. He walked over to the driver's side of the car and proceeded to remind Carolina to keep her eyes on the road and not talk with the passengers so she wouldn't be distracted. Pay attention to stop signs and traffic lights.

"Yes, yes, I know," she said, eager to get the show on the road.

"When the light turns green and you're first in line, don't take off immediately," he instructed. "Look to your right and left first."

"Chuy," she said, closing her eyes, "I *know* all of this."

We had four brothers, it was true, but sometimes it seemed we had four extra *fathers*.

"And here," he said, handing Carolina some dollar bills. "It's a three-hour movie, so buy yourselves some popcorn and whatever else you want." He turned to me in the back seat. "Happy birthday, Yoli bo-boli."

I waved to him, and he winked back.

Those three hours were wondrous. First there was the spectacular (there was no other word for it) opening as the novice Maria sang her signature song at the top of a hill, slowly turning with outstretched hands. I could barely catch my breath. And when she heard the church bells ringing—oops! late for midmorning prayers—and raced down the blooming meadow, I ran with her. Then when the Mother Abbess sends Fräulein Maria to work as a governess for Captain von Trapp's children, she falls in love with the captain, marries him, and—the grand finale—the family wins the folk festival contest just before slipping away, sneaking across the Alps to escape the war.

"Don't you think our family is just like the von Trapps?" I had asked Carolina and Ana as we'd filed out of the theater. I squinted, adjusting to the daylight. I was still up in the Alps, swooning with delight, the music in my head.

Carolina turned to me with an *Oh, brother* look on her face.

"We are!" I had insisted. "We have a big family and a bossy father just like them."

"Sure it's about a big family, Yoli," Carolina began, "but they aren't anything like us."

Ana had just shrugged as she got in the car. I could tell she wanted no part in what was starting to look like an argument between me and Carolina.

"It's just a movie," Carolina had continued. "I mean, it *is* based on a real family called the von Trapps and they *were* a singing group, but I bet it didn't all happen quite like that. You know how Hollywood movies are. It's called *poetic license*."

I felt like covering my ears. I'd wanted every bit of it to be true. The large family. The romance. The escape from Austria.

Instead, I gave Carolina a look and shook my head. Older sisters!

I refused to let Miss Negative Thinker get in the way of my love for the movie. For Christmas that year, Chuy bought me the original soundtrack album to *The Sound of Music*, and I wasted no time in memorizing all the songs. I sang them out loud in the privacy of my backyard. My singing breezed down Conifer Street, crossed Hollister Street, and sounded out to the Southern Pacific railroad tracks and over to the tomato fields. I liked to think that the hills being alive with the sound of my music would make the farmworkers' jobs a little less arduous.

So it was easy for me to sit on the three steps in the canyon and pretend it was the Alps and that on the other side was Switzerland instead of Interstate 5. I had a big, rambunctious family just like the von Trapps, and even better, tonight at dinner we were interviewing a governess who used to be a nun!

Well, she wasn't a real governess, and we weren't exactly interviewing her. It was more like Papá's cousin who happened to be an ex-nun. Even though she had never met us children, she had agreed to watch us while Mamá was in El Grullo in Mexico visiting my grandparents. Her father, my abuelito, was seriously sick.

I opened my diary: *March 31, 1967. I can't wait to meet her,* I wrote. *Is she as beautiful as Fräulein Maria? Did she leave the convent because she fell in love with a Captain von Trapp kind of guy? Because she decided to leave the convent, does that mean she'll try to discourage me from becoming a nun?*

Car sounds on the freeway competed with the cooing of mourning doves nesting nearby. I closed my diary and scanned my private Alps one more time. It had rained the day before—sloshy, mushy, pond-size puddles were everywhere. Once the mud hardened and dried, I'd be back here with Lydia, looking for trapdoor spiders.

I made my way up and out of the canyon to the empty lot. Checking Conifer Street for anyone who might be within hearing distance (the coast was clear), I sang "Do-Re-Mi" from *The Sound of Music* in my best operetta voice as I walked across the street to my house. I was singing to the eucalyptus and pepper trees, while the sweet pea blooms tangled in our front fence seemed to say, *Hurry up. She's coming soon!*

Opening the gate, I thought of all the fun things we'd do with our governess. Round and round I twirled toward the backyard, careful not to bump into the flowerpots, the brick borders of the flower bed, or the metal stilts of the three haughty flamingos. The birdbath.

My sister Ana was hanging the laundry on the clothesline and shouted for me to please shut up, my singing was, she claimed, doing permanent damage to her ears. She threatened to take one of the wooden clothespins and clamp my lips shut. *Besides*, she said, wasn't I supposed to be helping with the housecleaning?

Sometimes crabby sisters make it hard to live in the positive.

• • •

I went inside and Mamá put me to work cleaning the glass coffee table with Windex. I wiped it down and placed the crocheted doily back on the hairline crack in the middle. The plastic flowers in the vase on the table needed a good washing, too. One of us should've done that yesterday. No time now.

Papá's cousin had been a cloistered nun in Mexico but had recently left the convent. She was living with cousins in Tijuana, across the border, ten minutes away from us. According to Mamá, Tía Matilde was looking for a job, and when they asked was more than willing to stay at our house and watch over us while Mamá was away.

What would she think of the Sahagún estate? The first time Fräulein Maria saw the von Trapp residence, she was standing at the wrought iron gate, taking in the huge mansion where the widower Captain von Trapp lived with his seven children. Maria was probably thinking, *Whoa, horsey, this is no modest casita!* It was too bad she hadn't been standing before *our* gate. She would've felt right at home.

My Palm City neighborhood in south San Diego wasn't exactly in the same league as the von Trapps' neighborhood, but across the street from my house, we had an empty lot with a big bushy pepper tree, and behind the lot, the canyon. Our private playground. The famous Austrian family may have had a lake with swans and a romantic gazebo as part of their backyard, but we had the Pacific Ocean just a few miles west, with tons of seagulls. And it was true that we didn't have a gilded ballroom for Viennese waltzes, but we did have a patio in the back for Papá's impromptu Mexican hat dance renditions. Besides, how many times did the von Trapps play hide-and-go-seek under a full moon with *their* neighborhood friends?

TWO

Papá worked as a maintenance manager at a trailer park that required him to live on the premises during the week, but he'd taken part of today off so he could pick up his cousin and bring her to us. When he pulled up in front of the house, I was the first to spot them through the front window.

"She's here!" I shouted over my shoulder.

She stepped out of the truck and faced the Sahagún estate. A big woman—both in height and width—she wore a white cotton blouse, a pleated navy-blue skirt that hung modestly below her knees, thick black stockings, and low-heeled black pumps. A navy-blue cardigan rounded out the outfit. Her brown hair was firmly bound in a tight bun, and hanging around her neck was a gigantic wooden crucifix necklace. Kind enough smile, yes, but she was no Julie Andrews.

Papá guided his cousin into the house as he carried her small suitcase. We knew the drill when meeting a guest for the first time, and within seconds my four sisters and I stood in formation—oldest to youngest while Papá made his introductions.

"Girls, this is your tía Matilde," he said. It didn't matter how anyone was related to us. In my world, one of the millions of relatives we had was just as likely to be called tía as prima. Simple as that.

Then he introduced each of us.

"Carolina is the oldest of the girls," he reported as she stepped forward and shook Tía Matilde's hand. "She's in her last year of high school, and already quite the psychologist in the family."

"This is Ana María," he said. (We usually called her Ana, though she wished we'd use her full name because it sounded more grown-up.) "As you can see, she's the ugliest of the five." Big grin from Papá as Ana turned bright red. It was no secret (and obvious to anyone who bothered to even just glance her way) that fourteen-year-old Ana—with her long, dark curly hair and deep blue eyes, delicate nose, flawless complexion, and shy smile—was the beauty of the bunch.

"And this is Yolanda," he said with an exaggerated sigh (as if I were the problem child). "Twelve years old and already reads and writes like there is no tomorrow. I'm not sure what she is reading and writing, but let us hope it leads her to be the next Sor Juana Inés de la Cruz." And here he winked at me.

Why, why, why did he always have to compare me to the most brilliant, magnificent Mexican nun, a poet and scholar of the seventeenth century? His little joke, I supposed, but I didn't think it was funny.

I was hoping to catch his eye and glare at him, but he'd moved on to seven-year-old Monica, who, he revealed, loved horses and would become a famous Mexican charra someday. Next was Luz, the baby of the family, who was already showing, he said (and I agreed), a talent for art in her kindergarten class.

The only thing I could say in favor of these embarrassing introductions is that Papá had taught us to give firm, confident handshakes. And like Captain von Trapp, he looked on, satisfied with our greetings. All that was missing were his boatswain whistle and my brothers.

The three oldest were at work, and sixteen-year-old Tony was at a friend's house finishing a school report. They'd been excused from being present for Tía Matilde's arrival. Besides, they would have protested if our parents even insinuated that they needed a babysitter. But not so for Papá's five daughters—we needed utmost protection from the cold, cruel world of men and temptations!

My sisters and I followed Mamá into the kitchen while Papá was left to entertain his cousin. I could hear snippets of their conversation about the youthful days at La Lima, a ranch in Jalisco, when their grandparents had all the grandchildren visit during school holidays. Mamá, Papá, and Matilde had grown up in the town of El Grullo. But at eighteen, Matilde, who was younger than my parents, had entered the convent in the neighboring town of El Limón. I gathered from their talk about the good old days that they hadn't seen much of her since then.

"Those were good times, all right," Papá said, raising his voice to make sure we girls heard. "The kids of our generation, for one thing, were so much more respectful."

In the kitchen, my four sisters and I looked at one another.

"Yes," Tía Matilde said. "More respectful *and* more religious."

Uh-oh.

Suddenly I wondered if having Tía Matilde take care of us was a huge mistake. Wasn't our family religious enough? Mass on Sunday and Days of Obligation; our weekly family rosaries; and, during Lenten season, rosaries *daily* (as in the full forty days). Sure, I wanted to be a nun—someday—but in the meantime, couldn't she lead us singing in the hills, bicycling through the eucalyptus groves, dangling from pepper trees, and yodeling during marionette productions?

Once we were seated at the kitchen table, Papá at one end and Mamá at the other, with the rest of us squished on the sides, Papá turned to Tía Matilde and asked if she would do the honor of saying grace. "Con gusto," she said, bowing her head and proceeding to thank Nuestro Señor for this meal and this family. Her prayer was solemn and whispery, as if she and Our Lord had a special friendship. Would it be the same for me when I became a nun?

As Carolina and Mamá served the spaghetti, the adult dinner conversation was filled with pleasantries galore: Why had Cousin Teodoro's hip replacement gone wrong? Had Don Francisco died of too much drinking or because he was ninety-nine years old? Was it Doña Cuca or Petronila who'd had twelve kids and named them after the twelve apostles? Papá and Tía Matilde could not agree.

But then Papá wondered if dengue fever would hit El Grullo as hard this year as it had last year. The debilitating fevers, body aches. Even death.

Mamá and Tía Matilde shook their heads and sighed. One could only hope not.

"I wonder if there's a dengue fever problem in Vietnam," he added. "It's a tropical climate, too, ¿qué no?"

Nobody answered, but suddenly all the gaiety I had mustered this afternoon seemed to seep out of me, and in its place was what I'd been trying so hard not to think about: Bombs. Gunshot wounds. Dead soldiers. War. And Chuy. Would he be sent to Vietnam?

"God forbid that our son—"

"Lorenzo, please," Mamá said, giving him that look that said, *Basta. Enough of that talk.* Mamá didn't like us talking about Vietnam in front of her. *Pray*, she said whenever the news on TV switched to scenes of soldiers in jungles and coffins draped in U.S. flags on the tarmac. *Pray.*

"It is wonderful to finally meet you young ladies," Tía Matilde said, smiling at each of us. "I've heard good things about the Sahagún children."

A nice try on her part to change the subject to something pleasant, positive, but already my stomach was hurting.

"Gracias, Matilde," Papá said, pushing his plate away with a sigh. "We do the best we can to keep our boys and girls in line—all nine of them. Yes, indeed, Dolores and I have enough children to start a baseball team."

Oh, brother, here we go again. Aren't there groups of nine in something else besides baseball?

"And I'm looking forward to meeting the rest of the team," Tía Matilde remarked.

His sons were very independent, Papá declared, and so would not need much supervision. "Strapping young toros is what they are," he added.

I glanced at Carolina, about to turn eighteen years old and *pissed off*, as she put it, that our brothers—even Tony, who was younger than Carolina—could do whatever they wanted whereas *she* couldn't do anything under the watchful, strict eyes of our father.

Papá ignored her glare.

Once we cleared the dishes, Mamá brought out the flan.

And then my brothers bounded in—what timing!—front screen door opening and slamming shut, teasing and noisy clatter.

When they saw us at the table, they quieted down and stood—almost—in formation.

I was hoping, as we all eyed Papá's favorite dessert, that he might shorten their introductions so we could dive into the flan, but Papá seemed to relish these long introductions.

"Antonio," Papá said (though we called him Tony), "is sixteen and in love with this modern disque 'music'—at least *he* says it's music. I'm not so sure."

Tony stepped forward and shook Tía Matilde's hand.

Twenty-two-year-old Octavio had completed six months of active duty with the Marine Reserves a few years ago and now worked at Rohr Industries. "We hope his time in the reserves is all the military service he will have to do." Papá glanced at Mamá as Octavio shook hands with Tía Matilde, but she looked away.

Armando, at twenty-three, was the oldest, and a full-time student at San Diego State. "He worked at our neighborhood market, Brown's Market, for a year after high school to raise money for college," Papá explained with a proud grin. "Now he works there part-time and has just won a scholarship to study in Spain."

I was excited for Armando, but being away for a whole year was a long time.

Next Papá said, "And this is Chuy, who is twenty."

I had hoped he'd go on to say: *We are nervous that he will be drafted into the war. Please pray for him, Matilde, with all the nun prayers you have stored in you.*

Instead: "He works full-time at Brown's Market."

And this is one of the things I loved about my favorite brother. Unlike the other "strapping toros," Chuy stepped forward and bowed slightly before Tía Matilde. Then he took her hand in his and kissed it. "Jesús Manuel Sahagún Ramos a sus órdenes," he said with the kind of solemnity only a goofball like Chuy could get away with.

My parents were not amused, but we sisters pressed our lips together to keep from busting up.

"Fine, fine." Mamá quickly waved his nonsense away. Had they already eaten? "Pues bien, get a small plate and come have some flan."

You didn't have to ask them twice.

"Ah, Dolores," Tía Matilde said. "This looks delicious! Now that the whole family is here, might we say grace one more time before we have this lovely dessert?" She turned to me. "Yolanda, right?" she said. "I understand you want to become a nun."

"Yes," I said.

"Would you lead us in saying grace?"

I nodded. Yolanda Sahagún, future nun, was up to the job.

With the final *amen,* my brothers took their slices of flan and headed outside to eat on the patio. There wasn't room for us to all be together, and we always ate in shifts anyway, so the patio was fine with them.

I could see them through the window. They were laughing and joking, scarfing down the soft slices of custard in one or two mouthfuls. I would've liked to be out there, joining in their fun. Chuy was doing most of the talking, while the other three were grinning at whatever he was saying. Then a burst of laughter. He must've said something outrageously funny, because they were bent over in uncontrollable guffaws.

Not too long ago, Chuy wasn't laughing a lot. Robert Zuñiga, who he'd known since kindergarten, had been drafted to Vietnam. Three months in, Robert had been killed. I remembered how quiet and sad Chuy was for days. We all were.

Live in the positive, Miss Toscano said, but that was hard to do when the war could come knocking at our door any minute and take my Chuy away.

THREE

On Sunday, Lydia and I went searching for trapdoor spiders in the canyon. With sticks in hand, we looked for cork-like circles in the dirt that we would tap—*knock, knock*—to get the spiders to scurry to the top and peek out at us. You had to have super-keen eyesight to know where these camouflaged doors were. Lydia was usually a pro at finding them, but today we had no such luck. We tossed the sticks and headed to the pepper tree in the empty lot. We called it "our tree" and it was the perfect place for contemplating whatever we were in the mood to contemplate.

"What are your so-called governess's duties?" Lydia asked once we were sitting on the piece of plywood we'd jerry-rigged as a platform near the top of the tree. "Does she tutor you in academics or something?"

"Ha-ha," I said. "Mamá said Carolina and Ana should do the cooking. But after Mamá left yesterday, Tía Matilde said that she loves to cook, so she wants to help with the meals. She's going to get Monica and Luz ready for school and insists that she will walk the three of us to the bus stop in the morning, and then at noon she'll wait there for when Luz gets out of kindergarten. She agreed that when I get off the bus after school I can walk Monica home. So far, she seems to knit a lot and likes to watch whatever we're watching on TV."

"Is she nice?"

"Yes, she is," I said. "Really nice."

"So where do you all sleep?"

It was a fair question given that we had one small bedroom for all five sisters. My brothers also shared a room off the patio.

"Monica and Ana share the top bunk, and Carolina and Luz the bottom," I said. "Tía gets the single bed."

"And you?" she asked. "Wait! Don't tell me. The couch, right?"

"Yup," I said. "My own private bedroom, if you will."

She laughed. "That's one way of looking at it," she said. "Hmm, I wonder if we'll have our own private room in the convent or if nuns have roommates."

"What I wonder is why Tía Matilde left the convent after all those years."

"Why don't you just ask her?" Lydia said, swirling a Tootsie Pop in her mouth. Her tongue was purple.

"Mamá told us not to ask," I said. "She said it would be rude."

"Under normal circumstances that's probably true," Lydia said. "But since we're going to be nuns someday, we should know. Tell her that's why you're asking, so she doesn't think you're being a nosy metiche."

Lydia and I had been eight years old and preparing for our First

Holy Communion when we made our pact to become nuns. A Franciscan nun had come to speak to our catechism class at Saint Charles Church. I'd never seen such a saintly-looking nun. I was familiar with her habit: the headpiece, the veil, the black tunic, the wooden crucifix necklace. Where Papá had a jangle of keys hanging from his belt for his maintenance job, she had a rosary hanging from her waist. Her maintenance job was to pray for the poor, the sick, and the lost souls. As she passed out brochures to the girls detailing the activities at her convent, Lydia and I looked at each other with huge smiles. Our Lady of Angels in Glen Riddle, Pennsylvania (wherever that was), would be waiting for us with open arms. Since then, I'd kept the brochure with my diary in a shoebox that I hid in the toolshed.

Lydia was right: I should ask Tía Matilde why she'd left the convent. But I also knew I needed to wait for her to feel confianza in me to tell me the truth. That's why I planned to offer a saintly smile every time I said grace: I wanted her to think that I was not only an obedient and devout Catholic on the road to the nunnery, but that I was mature enough to be trusted with her story.

I'd been wanting to talk to Lydia about the altar boy at nine o'clock Mass—the one who lately had, as Carolina always said when she was interested in a guy, *caught my fancy*. When Father Carrasco made a corny joke during his sermons, Altar Boy's courtesy smile (surely it was a courtesy smile) revealed the cutest dimples. Did he look more like Davy Jones or Frankie Avalon? His mother was a member, like mine, of the church's group of parishioners devoted to celebrating the Virgen de Guadalupe. Mamá was the president of the Guadalupanas, and this allowed me to make some subtle inquiries about the families of these members. I had found out his name was Benjamín Sandoval, and he went to Saint Charles Catholic school. Sunday Mass was the only chance I had to see him. It seemed strange to me that I wanted to be a nun and that I had feelings about Benjamín.

"Do you think it's normal that I keep thinking about this cute altar boy at church?" I asked Lydia.

"Which Mass?" Lydia asked.

"Nine o'clock Mass with Father Carrasco."

"Oh, I know who you're talking about," she said, nodding. "He is a cutie pie, so I don't blame you."

"But if I want to be a nun—"

"Better to get it out of your system *now*, Yoli," she said, tossing the lollipop stick. "By the time we're ready to enter the convent, we will have had our fill of crushes and be done with the whole lot of them."

Sometimes Lydia was too mature for her own good.

"*We* will have had our fill?"

"Too bad ten-thirty Mass doesn't have interesting-looking altar boys," she said.

"*We*?" I said again. "Lydia, are you holding out on me?"

"Okay, okay," she said, shushing me with her raised hand. "Joey Fox. And don't you dare tell anyone, I'm warning you."

Joey was in our class at school, and I was surprised that's who had caught Lydia's fancy.

"Are you sure this doesn't mean we shouldn't be nuns?" I asked.

"Nah," she said. "We're going to make the best nuns ever. You'll see, Yoli."

I wasn't sure about *that*, but I was sure that when nine o'clock Mass rolled in next week, and a certain altar boy appeared behind Father Carrasco, my heart would—again!—skip a beat or two.

FOUR

"Did you hear about Martin Luther King's speech?" Armando asked Carolina on Thursday morning just before he headed out to classes at San Diego State.

I was in the kitchen packing my peanut butter and jelly sandwich for lunch.

"Mr. Griffith brought it up in civics class yesterday," she told Armando.

I knew exactly what they were talking about. Yesterday, Miss Toscano had written "Dr. Martin Luther King Jr." on the chalkboard and directed us to copy his name in our notebooks. "He is an important church and civil rights leader," she announced. "And he gave a speech about why he thinks the United States should not be involved in the Vietnam War." She seemed excited, like this was something we should be happy about and went on to talk more about what Dr. King said in his speech as well as his many accomplishments.

At the beginning of recess, I'd told Lydia I had to talk with Miss Toscano about something. Could she wait for me on the playground?

"Well, hurry it up," she'd said, glancing at the clouds. "It looks like it's going to rain, so recess might be cut short."

I went up to the teacher's desk. "Miss Toscano?"

"Yoli. What is it?"

"I was just wondering," I'd said, "about Martin Luther King and what he said in his speech."

"Have a seat, Yoli." Miss Toscano motioned to a desk in the front row. She came over and sat at the one next to mine.

"Do you think people will listen to him and the war is going to be over soon?" I had asked.

"I don't know, Yoli," she'd said, shaking her head. "You're asking because you have older brothers, don't you?"

I nodded and said, "I'm really worried about my brother Chuy. He isn't in college and he's twenty years old."

"I'd like to say that the government will listen to wise people like the Reverend King, and that the war will soon be over. But it's all so complicated." She'd looked at me with something like sadness in her eyes. "But I won't lie to you, Yoli. I have no idea when this will end."

I had thanked Miss Toscano and then walked out of the classroom and across the playground toward Lydia. She was frantically waving me over and pointing to the sky where somber dark clouds threatened a downpour.

• • •

Lydia and I were sitting on patio chairs on the front patch of my lawn on Saturday morning trying to decide whether to head for our tree or ride bikes.

Papá pulled up in his pickup truck, home from work. Even though he was a small, thin man, he was strong and good at repairing things—probably the best maintenance manager La Mesa trailer park ever had. He waved to us before entering the house. A few minutes later, Armando drove up in the blue Rambler.

"Pretty busy house," Lydia said.

"Tell me about it," I said. "No such thing as privacy. Why do you think I escape to the canyon?"

Lydia nodded as we watched Armando get out of the car. He'd be leaving in August for his year abroad in Spain, and the thing that stuck out in my memory when he was awarded the scholarship was overhearing Carolina whisper to Ana: "Student deferment. Thank God he'll be safe from the draft."

"What a dreamboat," Lydia said, once he was beyond hearing distance. She had decided that all four of my brothers—with their dark wavy hair and blue eyes, their *chiseled Romanesque features*, as she put it—were a cross between Elvis Presley and Little Joe of *Bonanza*. "I'll miss seeing him when he leaves," she added, sighing. "Thank God you still have three other brothers who'll be around."

"Lydia," I said. "You're grossing me out with your dreamboat stuff."

"C'mon, Yoli," she said. "Even you have to admit that your brothers are gorgeous." She batted her eyes. Silly best friend.

If I were to draw a little sketch next to my brothers' names on the shower sign-up sheet, for Armando I'd draw a picture of college textbooks and a map of Spain. Octavio's name would be surrounded by hearts and about a hundred stick figures of girls (our resident Heartbreaker, according to Carolina). For Tony, I'd draw round circles with a tiny dot in the middle of each, and inside the circles I'd write names like "Ray Charles" and "Motown" to represent his collection of albums and 45s.

And for Chuy? What would I draw for my favorite brother? I'd have to think about it.

"You're so lucky to have all these brothers, because they always have their guy friends hanging around."

"Jeez, Lydia," I said. "You sound kind of boy crazy for a girl who has plans to become a nun."

"Like I said, tonta, getting it out of my system."

"You must have some pretty long sessions in the confessional."

"Oh, yeah, always," she said. "And my penance is usually three hundred Our Fathers and ten thousand Hail Marys for the week."

"It sounds like you have enough sins to give mean old Father Carrasco a heart attack."

She looked at me, and we busted up laughing.

We decided to head to the pepper tree, and just as we settled on our platform we spotted Don Epifranio, an old widower who lived on our street, tottering along with Socorrito, our next-door neighbor and local gossip. Socorrito was Mamá's friend and had opinions about anything and everything, including the Vietnam War. I thought it was interesting that Mamá didn't want to talk about it and Socorrito was just the opposite.

Socorrito had her arm interlocked with Don Epifranio's and was talking a mile a minute while he nodded at whatever she was saying.

"Do you think they're in love?" Lydia asked. "Because if they are, they might as well just get married and move in together, even if they are old."

"They could be," I said. "I can see that between them." I looked up at the highest branches, sunlight peering through wherever it could. "Why not?"

FIVE

Tía Matilde had been with us for a month when Monica, Luz, and I asked Chuy and his best friend, El Chango, to drive us down Suicide Hill. We'd never been to Disneyland, and our measly annual Sun 'n' Sea Festival had one rickety roller coaster we weren't allowed to ride. But we had Suicide Hill just a few blocks away—a steep hill on Palm Avenue that most drivers avoided. And we had our brother Chuy, who had driven both our car and his bike down the hill. With Mamá out of town, he finally gave in to our begging.

Once there, Chuy, our pilot, told us to get into position. We leaned forward in the back seat as the Rambler chugged and strained its way up the steep incline. At times it seemed like the car was about to slide backward, but through some miracle—surely helped along by us three sisters leaning forward as instructed—we made it to the top of the hill.

Chuy turned to us and asked, "Are you ready, hermanitas?"
We nodded.
"And you?" Chuy said to his copilot, El Chango.
Another nod.

"Okay, then," he announced. "Get ready!"

El Chango clutched the dashboard, and my little sisters and I leaned back and held hands for added courage.

With Chuy's foot on the gas pedal, the car flew down the hill, and there was no stopping us. We three screamed bloody murder while El Chango laughed his head off. Seventy, eighty, a hundred miles an hour—who knew how fast we were going? The world outside was a blur of trees and fences and birds fluttering away. I squeezed my eyes shut. I was certain we were going to die or, at the very least, roll over and over into the unknown.

And when the car came to a screeching, abrupt stop at the bottom of the hill and I opened my eyes and saw that we were okay, that we hadn't died or crashed or rolled over, I began to laugh, too, exhilarated and relieved.

When we pulled up in front of our house, Luz and Monica scampered away, probably to brag to their little friends about having zoomed down Suicide Hill.

I thanked Chuy for the ride and headed toward the house. But then I heard El Chango ask my brother, "Did you hear they turned down Muhammad Ali's application to be a conscientious objector? They threatened him with jail, but he's fighting it."

Even I knew who Muhammad Ali was: the greatest boxer ever.

"What's a conscientious objector?" I piped in, not caring if they knew I'd been eavesdropping.

"Someone who objects to serving in the military because of moral or religious beliefs," said El Chango.

"You should apply for that, Chuy," I said.

"If the famous Muhammad Ali, with his high-powered attorneys, was turned down for CO," said Chuy, looking at me and then at El Chango, "what chance do I have?"

"But you should at least try," I said, glancing at El Chango, who nodded in agreement.

"I'll think about it," he said. "But if I'm drafted, hermanita, I'll go. I don't want to go to jail. We don't need to worry about it right now anyway—I'm starving."

El Chango glanced at his watch and remembered he had to get home and take his mom grocery shopping. Like Mamá, she didn't drive and needed one of the kids to act as chauffeur.

We watched as he limped away, up Conifer Street. I wondered if Chuy was envious that his best friend, with his polio-inflicted limp, didn't have to worry about being sent to Vietnam.

"If you can do scary things like bicycle down Suicide Hill at a hundred miles an hour," I said, hoping to get a smile out of him, "then applying for conscientious objector can't be any scarier, can it?"

"It's not that applying is scary, Yoli. I'm just not sure there's any point."

I looked at him, refusing to think negative thoughts. *Live in the positive* is what I had to do.

"And," he said, gently tugging on my braided pigtails before walking away, "I fly down Suicide Hill to feel the freedom, not exactly what I'll be feeling if I'm drafted."

As I watched him walk to the front door, I finally knew what I wanted to depict about Chuy on the bathroom sign-up sheet. But how would I draw the feeling of freedom?

SIX

Since she'd arrived, Tía Matilde had walked with me, Monica, and Luz every morning to the school bus stop. I kept telling her she didn't have to, that I could handle my whippersnapper little sisters, but she insisted. I still hadn't asked her about convent life, so I decided to broach the subject one morning when my sisters were running ahead of us toward the bus stop.

"I hope you don't mind my asking, but could you tell me what convent life was like for you?"

"I was a cloistered nun, which meant that I lived solely within the convent and rarely ventured out," she said. "But it depends upon what order you belong to."

I hadn't thought about being able to choose what kind of nun lifestyle I wanted. The Our Lady of Angels pamphlet that Lydia and I had received in catechism class had pictures of nuns out in the community, visiting elderly people and teaching in classrooms. Things like that.

"If you're cloistered," I said, "what do you do all day?"

Tía gave me a detailed itinerary of a day in the life of a cloistered nun: Prayers. Quiet, private readings of the Bible. Gregorian chants. More prayers—private and with the other nuns. A whole lot of housecleaning—or rather, convent cleaning.

"Hmm. Lydia wanted to know if you had roommates," I said.

"I did," she said. "But each convent has a different arrangement, depending on its size."

"I'm not sure what kind of order I want to join," I told her. "But, well, no offense, Tía, I'm pretty sure I don't want to be in a cloistered one."

Tía laughed. "I understand, Yoli," she said. "I really do."

• • •

I couldn't wait for summer vacation. I studied a lot because I wanted to "ace" sixth grade—as Armando would say—and when I wasn't studying I was daydreaming of daily tree climbing, trapdoor-spider hunting, rattlesnake spotting, and bicycle riding. I was the president of the Palm City Bike Gang because one day I'd declared to Lydia that we needed to be a gang of some sort and have an official name. She'd looked at me as if she'd just discovered I was cuckoo.

"Okay, okay. I mean *club*," I'd said, laughing. But we decided to stick to *gang* because it sounded more serious, tougher than *club*.

Lydia had insisted I be the president of the PCBG because I'd come up with the idea and had the loudest voice. It would easily carry in the wind to call out directions—"Head to the end of the alley!" "Sharp turn right on Hollister!" "Faster!"—as we pedaled along. We also decided that for it to be a gang—or a club for that matter—we needed more than two members, so every now and then we let ten-year-old Georgie the Pest from Citrus Street join us as well as Monica and Luz.

"Do you know how to ride a bicycle?" I asked Tía Matilde one Saturday as she watered the front-yard plants, the hose trailing her as she went from section to section.

"Bicycle riding was not something girls did growing up in El Grullo," she said. "And as a cloistered nun, I wouldn't have had reason to learn."

It was warm outside, and I was already dressed in my light blue summer pedal pushers and cotton blouse. Tía, on the other hand, was wearing one of her usual dreary-looking dresses, a dull brown sack of a thing. She wasn't in the convent anymore, and though she might be kind of old—maybe forty—and I would never say something to her about it, I couldn't understand why she didn't chuck the gloomy garb.

"I can teach you how to ride," I told her.

Tía Matilde turned off the hose. "Did you say you'd teach me to ride a bicycle?"

I nodded.

She wound the green hose into a tidy coil.

"Pues, bien," she said. "Why not?"

Sometimes people can surprise you.

Over the years, Saint Charles Church members had donated secondhand bikes to us. We had quite a collection from which

Tía Matilde could choose. For the first lesson, I had her straddle the bike but with her feet firmly on the ground. "Make friends with the bike," I told her. Chuy had said the same thing when he taught me.

"Yes, yes," she said, her face a study of determination. With her eyes narrowed and her lips firmly set, you would think she was preparing for her first-ever rocket launch to outer space.

I let go of the handlebar. Tía Matilde seemed caught by surprise. She and the bike nearly toppled over, even with her feet on the ground. She started making fun of her weight, certain that was why she couldn't balance.

"Even gorditas can learn," I reassured her.

She laughed. "Ah, so now you're calling me a little fatso, are you?"

"No," I said. "I'm calling you a lady who has been locked up in a convent for a long time and who is now going to learn to ride a bicycle!"

I put my hands back on the handlebars. We didn't say anything, just stared at each other. She was *my* apprentice, my bicycle student, and I wanted her to learn how fun it was to ride a bike.

"Yes, mi profesora," she said, saluting me.

And the lesson continued.

I had her sit on the bike and put her feet on the pedals while holding on to the fence for balance.

The next day after church we started in again. She seemed to be getting used to the bike—the handlebars, the pedals, the weight of the thing, the movement. There were still the self-conscious giggles, looking around her, making sure no one was watching as she pedaled forward a few yards with me at her side should I need to break her fall. We were still at it when Papá waved goodbye to us.

"Good luck," he said as he hopped in the truck and drove back to the trailer park.

If Fräulein Maria could ride a bicycle with her von Trapp charges, then by golly, so would Tía Matilde!

And then it happened on Monday after school, the miracle that I was praying for.

She was trembly at first, and I still trotted alongside. But then just like that—lotería!—she was on her way, a little faster, and I let her go ahead without me. Wisps of hair were happily escaping her tight bun, and her plump nalgas sat firm and determined on the seat. She made it to the end of the street before coming to a wobbly but respectable stop. I ran up to her.

She beamed. "This is so much fun, Yoli. I had no idea."

"You see?" I said. "Nunca es tarde."

Still breathless from her brief but successful takeoff, she nodded. Yes, it was never too late.

That was enough excitement for one day, we agreed. We walked the bike home, both of us feeling victorious.

I glanced at her. "When I first met you," I said, "I thought you were kind of a fuddy-duddy—una persona anticuada. I thought you'd be strict with us and have us praying all day long."

"What's wrong with praying all day long?" she said, smoothing the front of her sack dress.

Oops.

She laughed. "Just kidding," she said. "But is this the end of the lessons, then?"

"No, no," I said. "You need to practice so that you can get more confident."

"How can I repay you for your kindness and patience?" Tía Matilde asked.

I hadn't thought of this as a favor for a favor.

Then it came to me. "Tía," I said, "would you tell me the reason you left the convent?"

She looked at me, considering. "Yes, Yoli, I will," she said. "But not right now. I'm a bit tired from so much bike-riding excitement, and it's time to get started on dinner."

I wondered if she had lost faith in God and her religion—was that why she'd left the convent? No, it couldn't be that. After all, she still prayed. Had something happened behind the thick walls of the convent that made her question her vocation as a nun? Or could it have been, as I liked to think, that she had fallen in love, like Fräulein Maria had?

SEVEN

The last Saturday in May, Mamá called from Mexico to remind us that Tía Matilde's birthday was in three days. While Papá was home, she said, we should ask him for money to buy a birthday card and a present, and ingredients to make a cake.

That evening, as Papá settled in on the couch to read *El Mexicano*, one of his favorite Tijuana newspapers, we asked him for money. He set the newspaper down and fished in his pocket for his wallet.

"Here you go," he said, handing Carolina a few bills. "Make sure you get your tía something nice."

"I know just what to get her!" I later said to my sisters as Papá snoozed, his newspaper abandoned on his lap.

The next day, after church, Lydia and I took off on our bikes over to Kresge's. Within minutes, I had picked out a blouse with a bright yellow sunflower print and a pair of knit slacks, the hems bordered with the same sunflower fabric.

Lydia gave me a funny look.

"Tía's riding gear," I explained.

At home, Carolina sneaked me the birthday card when the coast was clear so I could sign it with a little note of appreciation.

"When are we going to give her the card and presents?" I asked.

"Yoli, just sign the card," she said. "I don't have time to discuss the birthday details. I still haven't decided if Betty Crocker and I are going to make a chocolate cake or a lemon one."

I opened the card. Already written were things like *Feliz cumpleaños, Tía. Thank you for putting up with us. Usted es tan simpática y dulce. We wish you many, many more birthdays.* Monica and Luz had wasted no time in putting to good use their sixty-four-crayon pack. Hearts and balloons dotted both sides of the card in Goldenrod, Forest Green, Lavender, Orchid, Turquoise Blue, Maize, and Periwinkle. I wondered if, like me, my little sisters picked the crayon for its name as much as for the color.

I stared at the card. Tía Matilde didn't have to sign up for shower times like we did, but if she *were* on the sign-up sheet, I knew exactly what I would draw next to her name. I sat down at the kitchen table and drew a bicycle, and riding it was a stick figure. And even though Tía Matilde wore her hair in a bun, I decided on something wild and free. I drew broom-like hair spiked every which way. Next to this exquisite work of art, I informed her that she was now an official member of the Palm City Bike Gang.

¡*Bienvenida!* I wrote.

• • •

Early Tuesday morning, we nine siblings assembled in the living room waiting for Tía Matilde to come out of the bedroom. She was usually the first to wake up, so this would be a double surprise for her: a bouquet of balloons and all of us awake before her. As she walked out of the bedroom yawning, Tony quickly set the needle on a record and "Las Mañanitas" began playing full blast. You would think we had a real, live mariachi in our living room!

"Ay, Dios mío," she said, laughing, her hands covering her cheeks, which were flushed red. "Oh, niños..."

And that was all she managed to say as her eyes filled with tears, the surprise birthday greeting a success. She hugged each one of us, shaking her head with emotion and disbelief. I could tell Tía wasn't used to this kind of fuss over her, not even on her birthday—and probably not in all the years she was a cloistered nun.

That evening, we presented her with the card and gifts and Carolina's chocolate cake. Papá called to wish her a happy birthday.

"Gracias, primo," she said, nodding into the phone while looking at us. "Yes, I am indeed enjoying my birthday like never before. This has been a most wonderful surprise!"

Listening to her say that made me feel happy that we'd made a fuss over her, but it also made me feel sad for what I might miss being in the convent.

• • •

On Saturday, Tía Matilde was in front of the house waiting for me. She had our bikes ready, like two horses hitched and saddled. Papá was just home from work, and I came out in time to see him get out of the truck and nod to his cousin.

"Well," he said. "That outfit is quite festive, prima."

Was that a smile he was trying to hide?

Once he went inside, Tía Matilde turned to me. "How do I look?" she asked.

She was wearing her new bike-riding outfit and looked like one big, bursting sunflower. She turned around slowly, deliberately. Maybe she was afraid she'd trip on her new tennis shoes (a gift from my brothers).

"Bellísima," I said, admiring my good taste in riding gear.

She laughed. "I doubt it," she said. "But it is very comfortable. You chose this, didn't you?"

I smiled.

"Thank you, Yoli," she said. "This is very special."

I picked easy beginner routes for her to cruise up and down—Conifer and Citrus Streets, which had little traffic. Her brown hair was tied in a ponytail. Every now and then I looked back to make sure she was close behind and that she hadn't fallen.

As we neared Georgie the Pest's house on Citrus Street, I called back to Tía Matilde, warning her that a dog was about to start barking. And sure enough, Georgie's grumpy old German shepherd bounded up to the chain-link fence and started barking as if he was about to take a bite out of us. I positioned my pedals midway and stood up and firmly shouted, "Quieto, Lobo!" He immediately stopped barking and began wagging his tail.

It was a sunny, blue June day—Lemon Yellow and Cornflower Blue?—with bits of scraggly clouds and a refreshing breeze brushing past us as we pedaled. I felt like I was the queen not only of the PCBG but also of my whole Palm City neighborhood.

We stopped at the end of Conifer Street and looked down the embankment at Interstate 5. The cars whizzed past. I could do this forever: stare at the cars, their whooshing sounding like waves. I could've filled the whole day with daydreams here and in the canyon.

I noticed Tía Matilde was doing the same.

"I wonder where they're going," I said to her.

"I wonder where they've been," she answered.

Then a police car swept past with its siren screaming, and we both watched as it headed north.

"I fell in love," Tía Matilde said, almost in a whisper.

I turned to look at her.

"When I was a teenager, not much older than you, before I'd even thought of entering a convent, I met a boy. His father was an agricultural engineer," she continued. "And the American company he worked for had transferred him and his family to El Grullo." She explained that sixteen-year-old Jeremy enrolled in the only preparatoria in town. "That's where we met," she said. She was smiling when she said this, and I could tell she was there and not here.

Their teacher ended up pairing Matilde with him because her English was the best in the class, and she could help him with translations until he became fluent in Spanish. Matilde and "Jeremías" became fast friends and were inseparable for the next two years.

Squinting, I saw her more clearly, what she must've looked like at sixteen with her light brown hair tied in a flirty ponytail with maybe a pink ribbon. Big hazel-colored eyes. Long, long eyelashes. A beautiful young girl.

There was, of course, lots of drama over their love. "Un escándalo," she said. Her parents had another boy in mind for her—a good *Catholic* boy she'd grown up with.

Tía Matilde had two choices: either run away with Jeremías, get married, and lose her family, or stay put and marry the boring, immature family friend.

And then it struck her that she had *another* choice: join the convent.

"I wasn't particularly religious," she admitted. "But if I couldn't marry my true love, I'd join the convent so I wouldn't have to marry the family friend."

"Couldn't you have just not married at all?"

"I suppose so," she said, laughing. "Maybe I was trying to punish myself for having been a coward and not accepting Jeremías's proposal to elope. Entering the convent was my penance."

"Were you pregnant?" I asked.

"Oh, no," she said, smiling sadly. "My story isn't *that* dramatic."

Sounded dramatic enough to me.

So before he and his family returned to the United States, Jeremías and Matilde made their heartbreaking plans: after they graduated from high school, she would become Christ's wife in a cloistered convent, and he would enlist in the army and fight in the Korean War, knowing that he'd probably be drafted anyway.

"He wrote me almost every day," she said.

I could imagine her reading those letters as she sat in her convent room after vespers. She'd be wearing her long black gown, his latest letter tucked in the fold of her side pocket, near her rosary.

"He mentioned very little about the war itself, the battles and all of that," she told me. "His letters were funny, and he purposely used Spanglish to tease me. He liked to combine the two so I could scold him. 'Yo te watcho when you get angry, and you are so bella,' he would say to me."

Eight months into his tour of duty, Tía Matilde received a call from his parents. Jeremy had been killed. And instead of resigning herself to this horrible turn of events—not questioning God's plan for him—she *did* question it.

"No," she said, shaking her head. "I didn't just question his plan; I argued with him constantly."

Jeremy's combat buddy telephoned her at the convent a few months later. He'd been with him the day he was shot. "He told me Jeremías talked about me all the time, was 'obviously, crazy in love with you,' were his words," she said, tightening the grip on the handlebars as if she were getting ready to ride down Suicide Hill. "His friend thought I'd want to know this, how much he'd loved me."

I could hear the three forty-five Southern Pacific blowing its whistle near Hollister and Palm. A long, lonely wail.

"This happened sixteen years ago," she said. "And yet…" She began weeping quietly and seemed to have lost her words. Or her heart.

Had I ever seen such sadness? Tía Matilde's true love was dead. The look in her eyes, the way her mouth was set—was this what heartbreak looked like?

"I later learned," she said through her tears, "that if we had married and had a child, he wouldn't have been drafted. He wouldn't have died."

I didn't say anything. What could I say?

"I had loved him so much, but because he wasn't Catholic…" She shook her head. "What a coward I was. I should've defied my parents and run off and married him. Instead, he died, and I no longer wanted to pray to God or even to ask him why," she said, glancing at me. "I had no business being a nun."

"But you remained in the convent for so many years after that," I said.

"Yes," she said. "Maybe I stayed in the convent to punish myself."

Lobo's deep, throaty barking in the distance brought me back.

As we walked our bikes to the house in silence, the sky turned a bruised purple—was there such a color in the sixty-four-crayon pack? I tried breathing evenly, calmly, but it was as if my own true love had just been announced dead on the battlefield. Turning into the yard, I glanced over my shoulder to my canyon, where I suddenly longed to be—hiding like a trapdoor spider or fleeing like a dove alert to the sound of a hunter's gun.

EIGHT

That evening, while Papá and Tía Matilde watched TV, I headed to the bedroom. I sat on the bottom bunk and filled in answers on the page titled "My Favorites" in my new autograph book. Sixth-grade graduation day was two and a half weeks away. I could hear Carolina, Ana, Monica, and Luz in the kitchen whispering among themselves.

Singer: Davy Jones
Movie or TV Star: Sally Field
Band: The Monkees
Song: "Last Train to Clarksville"
Food: Pan dulce (orejas)
Teacher: Miss Toscano
Sport: Bicycle riding
Subject: Reading
Favorite Girl Classmate: Lydia Hernández
Favorite Boy Classmate:

Hmm. I didn't have a favorite boy classmate, and I didn't want anyone, besides Lydia, knowing who my favorite boy was. Next to

Favorite Boy Classmate I wrote "AB." If asked, I'd say *All Boys* (though it was really code for *Altar Boy*).

My sisters' whispering grew louder, with an angry hiss now and then. Something was up.

I tiptoed to the kitchen. "What's going on?" I asked.

Ana and Carolina looked as if they'd just been caught sneaking an extra piece of pan dulce.

"What's all the whispering about?"

"Okay, fine," Carolina said. "This was supposed to be a surprise for you, but I'm going to tell you because we need your help."

"What, for Pete's sake?"

"Abuelito is doing better," Carolina explained, "so Mamá will be coming back in time for your graduation. I won't tell you exactly when she's going to arrive. I'll keep that a surprise. But we need to get the house in tip-top shape."

Mamá would be here for my graduation! I was happy about that, but there was one question poking at me like a thorn.

"Does that mean Tía Matilde will be leaving us?" I asked. "Will she be going back to Tijuana?"

"I asked Mamá about that," Carolina said. "She's going to try to convince Tía to stay with us and find work here in San Diego."

Oh, happy day! To have Mamá back and Tía still here with us—a double treat.

"Did you hear me, Miss Head in the Clouds?" Carolina barked at me. I laughed and nodded.

• • •

Carolina drove us sisters and Tía Matilde in the Rambler to early Mass while Papá drove his pickup with Armando and Tony. Chuy was at work, opening the store, and would join Octavio later for evening Mass. At the seven-thirty morning Mass, unfortunately, there was no sign of "AB."

I knew Sunday was supposed to be a day of rest, but today was packed with commands and activity, and I was happy to take orders from Miss Bossy Sister Commander because Mamá was coming home.

While Papá and Tía went to the Big Bear supermarket, the rest of us waited for Carolina's orders.

"What are you doing just standing there like a boba?" Carolina yelled at me. She sounded like she was *on the verge of hysteria*—a phrase I'd learned from her. "Get the mop."

"Aye, Aye, mi comandante!" I saluted her.

Our floor was vinyl squares, so at least I didn't have to vacuum like poor Lydia with her so-called shag carpet. While we sisters did most of the indoor cleaning, Tony was instructed to collect and put away his scattered albums and 45s from the living room. Armando was already gathering a bucket, soap, and clean rags to wash the Rambler, while Octavio pushed the lawn mower with its rusty blades over the square of grass in the front yard. Later, when Chuy got off work, he took it upon himself to wash the windows with the Windex spray bottle and old newspapers in hand.

"Newspaper to dry the windows?" I asked him as he cleaned the outside front windows. There were many news stories on Vietnam. Maybe using newspaper instead of rags was his way of physically crushing the news?

He nodded. "It does the trick." And to prove his point, he demonstrated by squirting the window with the blue liquid and then crumpling a page of newsprint to wipe the glass. "It'll leave ink on your hands by the time you're finished, but that's all."

Carolina, angry and scolding, shouted my name from the backyard. Chuy and I cautiously peered around the corner of the house as if we were about to meet up with a dragon. She was on the back patio, holding a broom and motioning like a loca for me to get over there. Quite the huffy regañona, that's for sure.

"Escoba detail for you, Yoli," Chuy said, smiling.

"Yup," I said, and headed to the patio.

Papá left for the trailer park, and that night at dinner Tía Matilde said, "You have all done a great job of cleaning up the house. As long as we keep things neat, we'll be ready for your mamá to return no matter when." Then she looked at me and winked.

• • •

The next Saturday, Lydia, Tía, and I went bike riding. With me in the lead, the three of us made a sharp right onto busy Hollister

Street. As we pedaled down the street, I thought about next week: only four more days of elementary school!

"U-turn," I shouted.

When we neared her street, Lydia called out goodbye and rode across the tracks toward her house.

Moments later, a little yapping Chihuahua chased after Tía's bike. Startled, she swerved and almost fell, but she caught herself in time and hightailed it out of range. We both started laughing—she looked so funny, this grown-up afraid of a tiny mouse of a dog! We were now on Conifer Street, and I slowed down to ride next to her so she could see my exaggerated imitation of her scared face, which made us crack up even more.

Arriving at the house, we hopped off our bikes as Papá's truck pulled up and stopped. His door opened, and then the other. There was Mamá!

I dropped my bike and ran to her. She got out of the truck and wrapped her warm, strong arms around me.

Then the front screen door opened and slammed shut once, twice, three, four times as my sisters rushed out. "¡Mamá!" "¡Mamita!" "¡Por fin!" "¡Bienvenida!"

A tangle of hugs and laughter as we talked, pushing and shoving our words on top of one another's. We had so much to tell her!

"Cálmense," Papá called out to us as he trailed behind, carrying her two pieces of luggage. "Your mother is tired, so take it easy."

We nodded. Yes, he was right. The three-day, two-night bus

trip from central Mexico to Tijuana would exhaust anyone. We made way for her to come into the house.

Then Mamá noticed Tía Matilde. "Matilde!" she exclaimed. "¡Qué transformación!" She gave Tía's sunflower outfit another look. "No me digas," she said. "Let me guess who had something to do with this." She turned to me, grinning. "Nice job, Yoli," she said.

My sisters and I, along with Mamá, Tía Matilde, and Papá, gathered in the kitchen. Tía insisted that Mamá and Papá sit at the kitchen table while she heated up some food for them.

"Matilde, that's not your job," said Mamá. "And I hope you haven't been the one doing the cooking." She gave Carolina and Ana a pointed stare.

"We tried to keep her out of the kitchen," Carolina said. "Honest. But that first night she insisted on making enchiladas suizas with tomatillos and... well..."

"She won us over," Ana piped in. "And, uh, took over."

"I love to cook," said Tía Matilde. "It was the one thing—maybe the only thing—I was very good at in the convent."

Carolina set the table, and Ana helped serve the rice and chicken with mole, another one of Tía's specialties. Soon the conversation turned to El Grullo town gossip.

"It seems many people hadn't known you'd left the convent," Mamá said. "They thought you were still there."

"Ah, that's too bad," said Tía, laughing. "Given that El Limón is not far from El Grullo, I assumed the news would've quickly reached El Grullo ears. If my parents had been alive, I'm sure it would've disappointed them. But *I'm* disappointed that my decision didn't cause an earth-shattering scandal."

How I loved my tía!

NINE

I stared in horror and disgust at my reflection in the mirror. Last night when I'd rolled my hair on the empty orange juice cans and torture-slept in them, I was expecting a sleek, straight-hair look today. But one hour before the graduation ceremony on this humid Thursday afternoon my hair was already shriveling up like pork rinds twisting and shrinking in the frying pan and turning into chicharrones.

I wouldn't have made such a fuss about it if it were just the graduation ceremony. Only Mamá, Tía Matilde, and my sisters were going to be there from my family, so no big deal. The problem—well, now it was a problem—was Suzy Johnston's graduation party. Our whole sixth-grade class was going, and Suzy's mom had invited a bunch of cousins and family friends—lots of cute boys, according to Suzy, many of them going to Southwest Junior High with us next year. Suzy had taken the liberty of telling the guys that she had the prettiest girlfriends this side of the Mississippi River.

"I'm not going to the party, and that's that," I said to Carolina and Ana when we returned from the short and boring graduation ceremony. "I hate my hair!"

"Well, the good news about your frizzy, curly hair," said Carolina, "is that when you become a nun, Yoli, they'll chop it off. With your nun's wimple, no one will ever have to see your hair again."

I ran into the bathroom and slammed the door as hard as I could. Stupid Carolina! She sure knew how to get to me. You would think that since she was about to graduate from high school, and going to her own graduation party next week, she'd understand.

I sat on the toilet-seat cover and cried. Just this once, just for today, I longed to have sleek, straight hair like all the surfer girls. Was this asking too much of God and the stars and the moon and the sun? Why, oh why, was I a miserable wreck of a girl?

"Yoli." I could hear Carolina softly knocking. "Yoli, come on out. I didn't mean it. I was just trying to make you laugh."

"Ha-ha," I shouted. "You are so funny I forgot to laugh! Just leave me alone. Get lost, all of you!"

"Yoli, I have a plan that's going to make you look even more beautiful than Gidget," she said.

I could hear whispering.

Could this be a trick? Would my four sisters be standing on the other side of the door ready to make more fun of me?

I slowly opened it.

The four were in the bedroom, waiting.

"I'm sorry, Yoli," Carolina said. "That wasn't nice of me to say."

"Apology accepted," I said.

"Okay, hermanas," she said, taking quick charge of the matter. "We need to get this young lady properly dolled up for the big bash." She led me to the dresser mirror. Five sister faces reflected in the mirror, about to embark on a mission of great importance.

Carolina and Ana proceeded to perform magic on my face and hair: first, a bright pink hairband. "Nobody will even notice your frizzy hair with this cute thing as your focal point," Carolina said. Once in place, the hairband did seem to take center stage.

Then Ana rolled my bangs around a small curler, bobby-pinned it, and sprayed it with a touch of Aqua Net. "That'll be the grand finale," she said. "You'll see."

"Because I love you, hermanita," Carolina said, reaching into her makeup bag, "and I don't want you to disgrace the Sahagún sisters by looking anything less than gorgeous at your first preteen party, here's Midnight Blue mascara for long, luscious eyelashes, and a smidgen of Pink Carnation for your lips."

Makeup for me! Ana wasn't even allowed to wear makeup yet (though she didn't need it—she was that pretty).

"When I graduate from sixth grade," Monica asked, "will you do this for me, too, Caro?"

"And me?" piped in little Luz.

"Of course, hermanitas!" Carolina said. "We will have nothing less than stunningly beautiful young ladies in this family."

I still had on my chiffon dress with its pink and blue flowers.

With the added pink hairband, it all came together nicely. And Ana was right about the curler. Once she took it off, my bangs sprang into place and stayed put on my forehead, hiding the four pimples underneath.

Carolina stood back and checked out her creation. "Not too shabby, hermanita."

We five walked into the living room, where Tía Matilde was knitting and Tony and Chuy were sitting on the floor, looking through Tony's album collection. On the coffee table was my Monkees record.

Chuy and Tony whistled at me, and my mother poked her head out of the kitchen. She beamed. "You look lovely, corazón."

"Hold on," said Tony. "We need a song for her send-off."

He picked up the Monkees album and put the record on the turntable. "I don't understand why you like them, Yoli, but here you go."

As the Monkees began to sing "Last Train to Clarksville," we five sisters moved our hips, snapped our fingers, and sang in unison. Mamá and Tía Matilde laughed at us, but what a show! With talent like this, we would surely win the next Austrian folk festival, just like the von Trapp family did.

As soon as it was over, Chuy grabbed the car keys from the top of the TV console. "Okay, Miss Last Train to Clarksville," he said. "Let's get the show on the road."

We hopped in the car, and he drove me to the party.

"Who all's going to be there?" he asked.

"My sixth-grade class," I said. "And some other friends of the Johnstons'. Miss Toscano, too."

He nodded. "Boys, too, huh?" he asked, putting on a pretend frown. "Like in *boyfriends*?"

"No," I said, and smiled. "Not boyfriends, just *friends*."

"Okay," he said. "I like the sound of that."

"Is Donna just your friend?" I asked.

He glanced at me, surprised. "I see you sisters have been talking about my love life."

"Oh, so she *is* your love?"

"Yup," he answered as he put on his signal to change lanes. "That's what she is all right."

I admired his profile as he looked ahead at the road. He had a slender nose, a strong, manly jaw, and blue eyes that seemed always up for fun travesuras. Lucky Donna.

"Chuy," I said, "can I ask you for some advice?" I felt embarrassed to ask but not that embarrassed. A guy's opinion might be exactly what I needed—especially Chuy's.

"Yeah, sure," he said, glancing at me as he continued west on Palm Avenue toward the beach. "Do you want brotherly advice or Dear Abby stuff?"

I laughed. "What's the difference?"

"Well, if you want me to be Dear Abby, then I'll be objective and come at it like a psychologist."

"You mean like Carolina?"

"Yup," he said. "But if it's *brotherly* advice you want, I'm going to come at it with some subjectivity, you know. I'll say whatever I need to say to protect you, hermanita. And the hell with psychology."

How I loved my brother!

"Can I have both kinds of advice?"

"Both?" he said, considering. "Okay, let's give it a try. Hit me with it."

"How can you tell if a guy is interested in you," I asked, "or even knows you exist?"

"Is this someone in your class?"

"No," I said. "That's the problem. He goes to another school."

"Have you ever talked to him?"

"Well, no," I said. "But I see him at nine o'clock Mass. He's an altar boy."

Maybe I should've just kept my mouth shut. I realized how stupid my situation was. But unlike my sisters, I knew Chuy would never tease me about my crush.

He looked at me. "Hmm, that's a tricky situation," he said. "Is there a mutual friend? Someone who could plan a little meeting between the two of you? If there is, maybe the three of you could go bike riding."

"No," I said. "There isn't a mutual friend."

"Let me think a minute." He turned left on First Avenue.

"Lydia's advice was for me to wait after Mass when he came out of the dressing area," I continued, "and casually say hi and remark on the interesting sermon Father Carrasco gave."

What Lydia had really said was that I should wait right outside the altar boys' dressing area, and as soon as he came out in his street clothes, I should go up and give him a big kiss on the lips, just like that. *Tell him you plan to become a nun*, she'd advised, *but you needed to get this kiss out of your system first.*

"*Interesting?* A Father Carrasco sermon?" Chuy said, laughing. "I like the first part: wait for him to come out. But I think you should be talking to our sisters, so it doesn't look like you're waiting for him. Have Carolina or Ana call out to him and ask him if he's going to next weekend's pancake breakfast. Maybe that could start a conversation."

I nodded, pleased. "Thank you, Chuy," I said.

"Hold on, I'm not finished," he said as he came to a stop at the red traffic light. "When you do talk to him for the first time, make sure you tell him you have four strong brothers who are very protective of their little sisters."

I smiled. "Is that the brotherly advice?"

"You bet," he said. "The most important part. Have fun, but make sure all the changos respect you, hermanita. No monkey business, okay?"

We were now turning up Suzy's long driveway. She was the only one I knew who had a circular driveway made of paving stones.

As I got out of the car, Chuy called, "A little fun before heading to the convent isn't a bad thing. Call me when you're ready to be picked up."

TEN

Suzy Johnston probably had the biggest house of us sixth graders, and her parents were known to be easygoing. They'd had a birthday party for Suzy back in January and pretty much let us kids have the whole house to ourselves, peeking in every so often to see if we needed any refills on fruit punch.

If my parents had hosted the party, there would've been three adult chaperones for every sixth grader, making sure no one got too physically familiar with anyone else. And the dancing? Naturally, Papá would have insisted I join him in a round of the Jarabe Tapatío.

I was sure Suzy's father would have enough sense not to embarrass her. And judging from the two-story brick house and columned front porch, Suzy and her parents, like the von Trapp family, would rather be doing a Viennese waltz than the Mexican Hat Dance.

At the front door, I was met not by Suzy or her parents, but by Lydia, who greeted me with a rush of breath: "Oh my God, Yoli! There are so many new cute guys! You're going to faint!"

Well! That sounded promising.

"You're still wearing your graduation dress?" she said, looking at me strangely as she led me in.

I followed her, noting how Lydia was wearing pedal pushers and a white summer blouse. *Poor thing, I should've counseled her on her clothing choice*, I thought as I straightened the pink sweater draped over my shoulders.

"Was that Chuy who dropped you off?" she asked.

I nodded.

"Darn, I should've come outside to meet you."

I admired the long circular staircase leading up to the bedrooms and bathrooms. Suzy was an only child, and though I wasn't particularly envious (well, maybe just a *little*), it did seem like a waste to have such a humungous house for just three people and a yellow Labrador named Reilly.

Lydia led me to the backyard, where tons of kids were hanging out. And if ever I wanted to die, that was the moment. Everyone was wearing shorts, slacks, or bathing suits. Even Miss Toscano, who was chatting with Suzy's parents, was wearing a pair of white slacks with a light blue blouse. I was the only one in a fancy dress. How fast could I dig myself a hole and jump in?

"Why is everyone in shorts?" I whispered to Lydia.

"The invitation said so," she said. *"Wear comfortable, summery clothes."*

I had just assumed that since Suzy lived in a fancy house, *summery clothes* meant nice, dressy clothes. I was a dorkus maximus.

There was an assortment of tuna, bologna, and peanut butter and jelly sandwiches, along with potato chips and dip and vanilla and chocolate cupcakes decorated with graduation caps on toothpicks. There was music playing—the Monkees, the Beach Boys, the Temptations, the Mamas and the Papas (and *no* Jarabe Tapatío). A couple of show-off guys cannonballed into the pool while most of us hung around the punch bowl taking swigs of tropical punch, pretending it was booze.

A classmate Lydia and I secretly called Mean Mary Ann sidled up to us, checking out my dress. "I see you're ready for prom night," she whispered to me. "Just six years too early."

She giggled and walked away before I had a chance to say something back.

Joey Fox and Antonio Ramírez came up to us. Antonio said he was going to Morelia to visit his grandparents this summer, and Joey (Lydia's crush) griped about having to go to Connecticut to visit relatives.

What about us—what were we going to do?

And that's when he walked in with two other guys.

Benjamín Sandoval.

Reilly wasted no time in bounding over to them, barking and making an excited ruckus (not unlike what my heart was doing), and Benjamín bent down to vigorously rub his muzzle, as if they were jolly old friends.

I thought I was going to faint, but instead I grew warm all over as if a fireball comet had flown right past my face. Here he was, fifteen feet away, wearing jeans and a light blue Hang Ten T-shirt with a pair of dark blue embroidered footprints on the breast pocket, near his heart. Suzy's mother went up to the three of them and said something that made them all laugh.

Lydia followed my stare. "Isn't that the altar—"

"Yes," I said in a choked-up whisper.

Joey asked Lydia something, and soon they were chatting, just the two of them.

"And what about you, Yoli?" Antonio asked. "What are you doing this summer?"

Benjamín and his friends headed to a group of guys who were manning the record player. Was I in a dream? Or was I really here in the romantic garden of a beautiful home, standing just feet away from Benjamín Sandoval?

"Yoli?"

I blinked and looked at Antonio. "Oh, what did you ask? Summer plans?"

He nodded.

"None," I said. "Just staying home."

Then it started to get dark outside, and someone turned on the party lights. Not the dumb Christmas lights my family used for summer backyard parties, but soft white lights casting everything in a silvery glow, like in a movie.

The cannonball swimmers came out of the pool, dried off, and headed into the house to change. A slight chill made me happy that I'd brought my sweater.

Suzy called out that it was time to dance.

The boys protested. "Ugh!" "Yuck!" "No way!"

Some of the girls giggled and glanced at one another, and then down at their shoes. I looked up at the heavens—oh, brother!—wondering where I could hide. It was bad enough that I was the only one wearing a party dress instead of comfortable summery clothes. Did I also have to bear the humiliation of waiting to see if some guy was going to ask me to dance? Well, one guy in particular. He was the only one I was interested in dancing with.

The Beach Boys started singing "California Girls," and a few guys and girls had paired up and were swaying to the beat. My, my, what was that? Joey was leading Lydia to the middle of the patio to dance. I figured I'd better prepare myself for her nonstop yakking about it the rest of the summer.

"Yoli?"

"What?" I had completely forgotten Antonio was still standing next to me.

"You wanna dance?" he asked.

"Uh, thank you, but I'm feeling a little queasy right now."

He nodded an okay, and wondered if crackers would help.

I motioned with my head to a group of girls at the other end of the patio. "They're making goo-goo eyes at you," I said.

"That's true," he said, laughing. "I better not disappoint them. See you later." And he was off in their direction.

Benjamín started browsing through the stack of albums. I wondered who his favorite groups were. Maybe I should inch my way over there and casually *ask* him. God, no, I didn't want to seem like I was chasing him.

If this was the best of it, I wouldn't complain. To gaze at him all evening like a secret admirer, maybe that was my lot in life.

And then Suzy was there, next to Benjamín, laughing at something he was saying. She reached over and touched his arm. With her shiny blond hair in a smart bob, Suzy always looked put together. Today she was wearing khaki-colored Bermuda shorts, complemented by a white dotted-swiss midriff blouse with a line of pompon balls dangling along the hem. I glanced down at my dress. I looked like some ancient Aunt Abigail ready for Easter Sunday Mass in 1948.

I inched backward, one step then another, pulling away from the party and the lights. There was much chatter and laughing, occasional playful Reilly barks. Nobody would notice my retreat.

Moving around the pool, I headed toward an expanse of lawn so large I was expecting any minute to come upon a gazebo like the von Trapps'. The perimeter was bordered with pristine roses in full bloom. I moved in closer to smell one, and as I did, I felt something soft and mushy under my shoe.

Oh, crap! Thank you very much, Reilly. I stepped back and tiptoed away from the area, scraping the sole of my shoe against the grass.

No way could I go back to the hubbub of the party smelling like this. I wanted to disappear, escape into the Twilight Zone—or, wait! Maybe this *was* the Twilight Zone.

Spotting a lone garden bench near a camellia bush, I headed that way, searching for a stick or something that would aid me in cleaning my shoe.

I sat down and decided to just break off a camellia branch. "Sorry, old girl," I whispered to the bush.

As I scraped the sole of my shoe, I wondered if I could get to the bathroom unnoticed, wipe the rest off with toilet paper, and then go home.

"Even with poop on your shoes," someone said, "you're still the prettiest girl here."

I looked up and there he was, Benjamín Sandoval, talking to *me*.

There'd be that moment—maybe next week or two months from now—when I'd think about this night and wonder if I'd made it all up. Had it just been part of my von Trapp family fairy tale? But if I *had* made it up, I would've added a lake in the background with two white swans swimming past just as Benjamín spoke to me. We'd be sitting on a bench in an expanse of lawn on a summer evening, and suddenly the crackle of thunder and big drops of rain would have us running to the glass gazebo for shelter. Like Liesl von Trapp and her beau, Rolf, Benjamín and I would begin singing and dancing.

The party could've gone a hundred ways, but I never for a moment thought it would go in my favor.

Even with poop on your shoes, you're still the prettiest girl here.

My face probably turned a hundred shades of red. And when he said, "Hand me your shoe," and took it from me, I thought I was going to faint. I blinked a couple of times.

Holding my stinky shoe in one hand, Benjamín glanced around and spotted a spigot I hadn't noticed. He turned it on, and a steady trickle of water washed off the remaining gunk.

I watched from my spot on the bench as he turned off the spigot and wiped the wet sole against the grass to dry it.

"Like new," he said, handing me the shoe.

"Thank you." At least I managed that.

He smiled. Definitely a Frankie Avalon–type of guy, with his dark hair and dreamy smile.

"I'm Benjamín, by the way," he said.

"Mucho gusto," I answered automatically. (Dumb, dumb, dumb. Papá had us too well trained in introductions). "Uh, I'm Yolanda, but everyone calls me Yoli."

"El gusto is mine, Yoli," he said, grinning.

Then, making himself at home next to me on the bench, he said, "I'm not a big fan, either."

"Huh?" I asked. "What?"

"Father Carrasco," he said. "I've counted at least five eye rolls a sermon from you."

"Only five?" I said, laughing. Thrilled. So he *had* noticed me!

"He can sometimes be real bossy, even to us altar boys. Like we're his servants or something."

"I'm not surprised," I said.

"My older brothers were altar boys," he said, sighing. "So now it's my turn."

"Oh."

"I notice you receive Communion every Sunday," he said. "Does that mean you go to confession every Saturday?"

"No," I said. "I go every two weeks or so, depending on how I'm doing with my sins."

He nodded. "My teacher, Sister Marie, thinks we should go to confession every week—for a weekly soul cleansing, she calls it—whether we need it or not."

"And do you?" I asked, realizing that this was an odd thing to be talking about right off the bat when meeting a boy. Confession and sins.

"Do I what?" he asked. "Need it or *do* it?"

I smiled. "Both, I guess."

"No and yes," he said. "I do it, you know, go through the motions, get in line with the rest of the class on Friday morning for the Saint Charles Catholic School confession special, but I think it's stupid to go every week when you don't have any big sins to tell."

"So then?" I asked.

"So I make them up," he said.

"Like what?"

"I usually start by making up stuff about disobeying my mother, and then I end by saying I cussed at my brothers. Hey, I even say the cuss words to see if Father Carrasco reacts to them."

"And does he?"

"Nah, nothing from him other than ordering me to say a rosary," he said. "I get the feeling he's asleep on his side of the confessional."

After that we sat on the bench for a long time without saying another word. From our spot at the far end of the garden, we could hear the constant chatter and laughter of the others on the patio, a few goofballs singing in falsetto along with the record player.

And then—darn it!—Lydia was calling my name.

I pretended not to hear. I wanted to sit next to Benjamín on this bench in this twinkling garden forever. But Lydia had a loud, high-pitched voice. "Yoliiiii," she called again, as if she were yodeling in the Alps.

"Well," I said finally. "I'm being summoned. I guess I better go."

I got up and so did he.

"Maybe I should go first," I said. "You know, alone."

He looked at me, confused. Then he smiled. "Oh, I see," he said. "Gossip."

"Thank you," I said. "You know, for the shoe and all."

"That's okay," he said, and nodded.

"I mean, really," I said. "That was very nice of you."

"Just being a good altar boy," he said. "Even when I'm off duty."

"This good deed should absolve you of all your wretched sins for the next week," I said.

"God, I hope so!" He smiled at me. Dimples, gorgeous dimples.

"Hey, uh," he said, "any chance I can see you again?"

Oh, heart, calm down!

"Sure," I said. "Um, let's see... How about two o'clock some Sunday at the bench across from Brown's Market?" I suggested. That was the time Papá was usually busy with last-minute chores at home or taking Mamá to run errands before he had to leave for the trailer park.

"Just give me a nod during Communion," he said as I turned toward the lit-up aqua pool, the twinkling lights, the laughter, and music.

And that was that.

"I wanted to say goodbye," Lydia said when I caught up with her. "My dad's in front honking the horn. We're going to L.A. tonight to stay with our relatives." Then she stopped and stared at me like she was a doctor examining my face. "Man, your face is all red, Yoli, and I have a feeling I know why." She gave me a goofy wink. "Let's talk about your altar boy when I get back."

A quick hug and she was gone. Yes, we had a lot to talk about.

ELEVEN

"Some guy just called for you, Carolina," my father announced Saturday when we sisters were all sitting at the kitchen table finishing our bologna sandwiches.

"Who?" she asked.

"I don't know," he said. "I told him to never call again."

"Oh, you did, did you?" she said. "And what did *he* say?"

"Nothing. I hung up on the chango, of course," Papá said, annoyed that he had to answer the obvious.

"Chango?" Carolina said. There was a spooky calmness to her voice. "Why are all guys monkeys to you?"

Nothing from Papá.

"You just hung up on the guy without even asking what he wanted?" she said.

"I most certainly did." Papá cleared his throat. "This evening I want all of you ladies home," he said. "We are going to talk about our household rules."

"What about our brothers?" Carolina asked. "They need to be here, too, right?" Whatever she had learned in her Mexican American Club in high school seemed to be making her braver. *Equal rights,* she had recently said to us sisters. *That's what we need around this house. Equal rights.*

"Yes, fine," he said. "Them, too." Papá turned to us. "What are you all looking at?" he demanded. "Don't you have things to do?"

We scattered. There were wars and then there were wars. I was excited for the next battle and proud of Carolina. She was the oldest sister, so it made sense that she'd have to break the ice, as she called it. Once she did this, phone calls from guys would be easier for the rest of us.

• • •

Later that evening the Sahagún family gathered in the living room—a rare occasion for all of us to be together in one room at the same time. Tía Matilde, after much coaxing from Mamá, my sisters, and me, joined us, too.

"Fine," she had finally said. "I'll join you, but with the understanding that I am only a spectator. These are family matters, and I have no business interfering."

Maybe if Tía Matilde had had older sisters to fight for her love rights, she could've married her Jeremías.

I loved these family conferencias, the fact that we were all assembled. Captain Sahagún, standing before his crew, called us to order by tapping a pen against a drinking glass and clearing his throat a few times.

"Get ready for his theatrics," Carolina mumbled.

And then: It had come to his attention—by pura coincidencia—

that one of the house rules wasn't being followed. "Phone calls from boys to you girls are strictly prohibited until you reach the age of twenty-one," he said, looking at us five. "The other thing I want to talk to you about is—"

"Excuse me," Carolina said, quickly raising her hand. "I think we need to revisit that rule."

"There is no revisiting," Papá said. "These are my rules and this is my—"

"*Our* home," she said.

His blue eyes stared at Carolina's, as if they knew the fight was about to begin.

"*My* house!" he shouted. "And there will be no discussing or arguing—"

"There's a difference between a house and a home, Papá." Carolina gave him a look I knew well: she wasn't backing down.

"I don't know what disparates you're saying," he said. "Don't play games with me, Carolina."

"Yes, this is your house, Papá, I won't deny that," she said, and nodded. "This, shall we say, little casita you bought is yours and Mama's."

I glanced at my mother. She was trying hard not to smile, but her green eyes seemed to dance with pride. I turned to Chuy and he winked at me.

Papá attempted to continue. "Rule number two—"

"But a home," Carolina interrupted, "now, *that's* a different thing. A home is an emotional and psychological space defined not so much by walls and a roof, but—"

"What the devil are you talking about?" he shouted. "Casa, hogar—it's all the same thing, and I am the one who makes the rules—"

"In your *house*, Papá," she said, interrupting him again, "but not in a *home*. We live in a democratic country, not in some Latin American dictatorship, so I believe we should make these rules together—for the sake of creating a healthy *home* environment."

He stared at her, his face flushed.

"I would like to suggest that we all get to talk with our friends on the phone—male or female—as long as we let you and Mamá know who these friends are," she said.

"That sounds very reasonable, Papá," Armando piped in.

Papá shot him an angry glance, but Carolina jumped in again.

"Thank you for your support, Armando," she said. "But this asunto is between me and Papá. I'm the oldest daughter, as you are the oldest son, and it's up to us to forge a democratic road for our younger siblings. But in this case"—she now directed her attention to our father—"it is up to me, as the oldest sister, to help create a home environment where justice and equal rights are given to the daughters. We should be allowed, as you are, to receive calls from girls *and* boys."

At first Papá didn't say anything, and that was a good sign. Even his face had turned back to its normal color. I had the feeling he was secretly impressed with her little speech.

"Pues, Carolina," he said. "You do bring up some interesting points."

He looked at her, then at each of us. Were we all holding our breath?

Then: "Fine," he said, sighing. "I will grant that."

"Thank you, Papá," Carolina said.

I couldn't wait to take Psychology 101 when I got to high school.

"Now can we move on?" he said.

Everyone nodded.

"I wish to discuss the length of phone calls to your friends," he said. "And this applies to *all* of you." Suddenly grinning, he pulled out a folded piece of paper from his shirt pocket, as if this was the grand moment he'd been waiting for. Tired of busy signals every time he tried to call home, Papá explained, he had drawn up a contract that we nine children were to sign, pledging that we would not be on the telephone for more than three minutes per call.

We brothers and sisters glanced at one another.

Three minutes?

Nobody could have a decent conversation in three minutes! Papá might as well have announced that he was yanking the telephone cord and tossing the phone out the window.

"Here it is," Papá said as he handed Carolina the contract.

I sidled up next to her and read the miserable thing as if it were our death decree.

Our names, typed with a line next to each for a signature, were in order of age. Armando's was the first one, followed by Octavio's and down the line to the rest of us.

Carolina read it and then looked up at Papá. "I would like to suggest a compromise," she said. "I think ten minutes is a more reasonable time, but I think we might be willing to settle for six minutes."

She looked at each of us for confirmation. We all gave her a vigorous nod of agreement and gratitude for her negotiating courage.

"That's three minutes more than what I've proposed," he said.

"And four minutes less than what we want," she answered.

He looked at each of us, his finger tapping his chin to emphasize that he was giving this great thought.

"Bueno," he said. "Ni tú ni yo." He pulled out a pen from his shirt pocket, took the contract from Carolina, and crossed out *tres minutos* and wrote in *seis minutos*, along with his initials.

He handed his contract to Armando, who passed it around for each of us to sign. I wondered if I might be able to coax Papá to pick up an imaginary guitar and sing the "Edelweiss" song like Captain von Trapp did. But studying his firmly set mouth, I decided *Never mind*.

When it was Luz's turn to sign, she dashed to the bedroom and returned with her box of crayons. She wrote her name in chunky, blocky kindergarten letters with the pen, which she also used to draw a square with an A-frame roof, two windows, and a door, as if she'd been practicing all year long at school to draw a house. Then, digging into her treasure trove of crayons and finding what she needed, she added Goldenrod beams radiating from and illuminating our home.

Luz. Light.

TWELVE

This morning at nine o'clock Mass, I'd been tempted to give Benjamín the nod. But Suzy's party happened just a few days ago, so wasn't it too soon? I'd overheard Carolina and Ana, at least a hundred times, discuss strategies with their girlfriends about boyfriends—that is, if they ever were to have a boyfriend. Given how strict Papá was on that subject, they'd probably be little old ladies before they could date. But that didn't stop them from devising strategies: *Play hard to get. Don't seem too eager.* Their voices sounded solemn and full of warning, as if being too eager would be disastrous and ruin their lives. I never understood why, and I couldn't ask them because then they'd know I'd been listening in.

From my perch in the canyon, I stared out at the freeway. Lydia was still in L.A., so I hadn't had a chance to tell her what all happened at Suzy's party. Besides, that night she had goo-goo eyes for Joey. They'd actually danced together, while all I could offer was that Benjamín had cleaned poop off my shoe.

I looked up from my diary when I heard my name being called. It sounded like Carolina shouting. I jotted down one last thought:

Play hard to get and don't seem too eager—whatever the heck that means, Dear Diary.

• • •

"Okay, Yoli," Carolina said, greeting me at the front door with a big grin on her face. "I'm about to tell you something that is probably going to have you swooning with delight."

I wasn't in the mood for her games.

"The love of your life came knocking at the door about thirty minutes ago asking for you."

"Huh?"

"Oh, yes, indeedy," she said. "Your angel baby, your sweet altar boy with the cute dimples came a-calling."

Was my crush on him that obvious that my sisters had figured it out by watching me at church?

"Sure," I said. "Whatever." Carolina's teasing could be so annoying.

She grinned like a tonta.

"You know, Carolina," I said. "You may think you're funny and all, but I'm not in the mood for your jokes. I'm not bugging you, so could you please—"

She didn't let me finish. She called out to Tía Matilde.

Yes, Tía Matilde confirmed, the altar boy had stopped by on his bike, asking for me.

"Why didn't you tell him where he could find me?"

"In the canyon?" she said. "No, no, no! He needs to work at this a bit. Can't make it too easy for him. But because I love you, my skeptical hermanita, I did you the favor of giving him our phone number. I told him to call before eight o'clock—before Mamá and Papá get home from Tijuana."

Papá and Mamá sometimes enjoyed going to the popular Mercado Hidalgo on Sundays for groceries and then stopping for a bite to eat. After such days, Papá would go to the trailer park extra early Monday morning instead of Sunday night.

Even though I was pretty sure Mamá would be okay with me chatting for a few minutes on the phone with a guy, Papá might not be—I wasn't sure that the new phone rule applied to twelve-year-old me. Carolina must have been thinking the same thing.

"And because I really, really love you, we are not going to tell Papá you got a phone call from a guy. And don't forget: un máximo de seis minutos," she said, imitating Papá's manly voice.

Carolina said I'd be swooning with delight. How about heart palpitations and a swirl of billowy clouds circling above my head like a halo? Any minute I'd be levitating.

I got through dinner and dishes and sweeping the kitchen floor, but by the time the call came, I had no recollection of ever having done any chores. *Discombobulated* was my new favorite word.

"How are your party shoes doing?" Benjamín asked right off the bat. "Have they gotten into any stinky messes lately?"

"Nope," I said. "But I know someone who is an expert at washing off stinky messes."

He laughed, then said, "The reason I'm calling is that I was wondering if we could meet up next Sunday."

"Uh, yeah, I'd like that," I said, my heart about to jump out of my body. "I have to ask permission, but I think I can."

"Good," he said. Was that a sigh of relief I could hear? "My family and I are going to visit my abuelitos in Mexico in July. We go every year, and we stay the whole month, so I was hoping we could meet before I left."

How high could I fly?

When I got off the phone, I turned and saw that all four sisters and Tía Matilde had been huddled in the kitchen, trying to hide from me, but well within hearing distance of my phone call.

"Okay, metiches," I said, beaming. "You can all come out now."

"And so?" said Ana. "What'd he say?"

I grinned at the five of them. "If you don't mind, ladies," I said, batting my eyelashes, "I *do* have a private life the likes of you busybodies are not privy to."

They started laughing.

"Look," little Luz said, giggling. "Yoli's face is all red!"

• • •

"You can meet him for thirty minutes, Yoli," Mamá said to me in private when I had asked her for permission. "His mother is a fellow Guadalupana member and very devout, and he is an altar boy, so I trust you two."

I was relieved that she had given me permission.

"But I think your father does not need to know," she added. "There is enough family drama without another *conferencia* taking place to discuss this."

Sunday couldn't come soon enough, but when it did, I was ready. I gave Benjamín a nod during Communion to let him know we could get together. And thanks to my sisters' intervention, I was wearing navy-blue Bermuda shorts and, after trying on ten blouses, we agreed on the floral print with a row of pearl buttons down the front.

"It's feminine and dainty," Ana said. "Without it screaming *I'm yours! I'm yours!*"

Luz thought I should arrange my hair in two braids, while Monica thought a ponytail would be more fun. But Carolina stepped in and said, "She's not a child anymore, so let her wear her hair down."

"It's more romantic," Ana noted, "without it screaming—"

"Yes, yes, we know, Ana," said Carolina. "You've made your point."

Mamá was out with Papá, so I turned to Tía Matilde. "Do I look okay?" I asked.

"You look lovely," Tía said, giving me a kiss on my forehead. "May God bless you and keep you safe."

As I turned to leave, she said, "Oh, wait! Don't you need a chaperone?"

I was about to open my mouth and protest. "Just kidding," she said. "Pero pórtate bien."

Yes, yes, of course I'd behave.

• • •

As I rode my bike the two blocks to Brown's Market, I pedaled with extra gusto.

I could see Benjamín in the distance waiting for me at the bus stop, so I quickly slowed down. *Act cool, Yoli, not too eager.*

"Watch it!" I heard him call out just as I headed toward a huge pothole in the street. The bike skidded and I tried keeping it upright, shifting my weight against gravity. But both the bike and I fell over, smashing into the ground in the most not-cool way.

Benjamín came running.

"Are you okay?" he asked, lifting my bike with one hand and taking my arm with the other.

Gravelly imprints on one elbow and a bit of blood on my knees, but I was okay.

"Uh, yeah, I'm fine," I said, glancing at the pothole that had caused my fall, wishing it were a little deeper so I could dive in and never come out.

He walked my bike, leading me to the bus stop bench. "Why don't you sit here while I get us some sodas. What would you like?" he asked.

"I'd like a 7UP, please."

"Should I get some Band-Aids, too?"

I shook my head. "Nah, it's no big deal. But thank you."

While he was in Brown's Market, I had a chance to gather my wits. I brushed off the gravel and took a tissue from my pocket to dab at the blood on my knee. Jeez. First, stinky, poopy shoes—and now this. He must have been thinking I was the biggest klutz in the world.

He returned with our cold, uncapped bottles of soda.

"Thank you," I said as he handed me the green bottle. "Doctor Pimienta for you, I see."

"You're not a fan?"

"Not really," I said. "Too spicy or something." *Dumb, dumb, dumb.*

"Dogs or cats?"

"Dogs!" I answered.

"Baby Ruth or—"

"Almond Joy!"

"Beatles or Rolling Stones?"

"Really?" I said, laughing. "You have to ask?"

There was a row of eucalyptus trees behind us, shading our cozy spot on the bench. We took sips of our sodas.

"Where in Mexico do your abuelitos live?" I asked him.

"In Guadalajara."

"That's a big city," I said. "Lots to do and see."

"Yeah, but mainly we have to sit at the dining room table talking to my grandparents for hours every day."

I laughed. "Same with me when we visit my abuelitos in El

Grullo," I said. "A lot of eating and hearing about the town's gossip and news. Most of the time it's boring. But sometimes my relatives and the neighbors have an interesting story or two about the good old days."

"Hey, speaking of news, did you hear that Palm City Go-Karts is opening soon?"

"I love go-karts," I said, as if I were an expert on them. I wasn't, but I quickly explained that my brother Chuy had built one a couple of years ago and had me test-drive it. "He wanted to see how fast it would go. I was the lightest while still being tall enough to touch the pedals, so he picked me."

"How fast did it go?" he asked.

"I don't know," I said. "But fast enough to have me crash into a parked car's tire and leave me with a nice little gash on my leg."

"Oh, wow," he said. "That must've hurt."

I pointed to a three-inch scar on my shin. "My badge of honor," I said.

"Hey, I have an idea. If the go-kart place is open next time we meet, how about if we go there?" Benjamín said.

Next time we meet.

"Yes," I said, trying not to show too much excitement. "That sounds like a fun idea."

"Next stop: go-kart riding!" he said. "You can demonstrate some of your daredevil driving."

My thirty minutes were up and, though I wished we could have talked all afternoon, it was time for me to leave.

"Well," I said. "I have to go." I got on my bike and tapped the kickstand with my foot. "Have fun visiting your abuelitos."

"I'll try," he said as he stood up and waved to me.

I waved back.

"Hey, Yoli," he called as I was about to ride away.

I stopped and turned to him.

"Next stop: go-kart riding!"

I grinned. He'd already said that.

"I already said that, didn't I?"

We both laughed. My face was probably the same shade of red as his. He'd be gone a whole month, and already I was missing him.

THIRTEEN

"I'm back," Lydia said the next morning as soon as I answered the phone. "And I want to hear all about it."

"Good morning to you, too," I said. "And why are you calling so early? Even the roosters aren't up yet, Lydia."

"It's eight o'clock in the morning," she said. "And if there were roosters around, by this time they'd be out flirting with the hens. How soon can we meet to hear about *your* rooster at the graduation party?"

"Jeez, Lydia," I said, laughing. "A bit more gentility, please."

"All right, all right," she said. "Do you want to meet at our tree at noon?"

When I got there, she was already waiting for me. I figured she had exciting romantic things of her own to share about Joey Fox.

"No, not really," she said in answer to my question.

"But you were dancing together."

"Yeah," she said, and nodded. "But as soon as the song was over, he thanked me and then rushed off to ask Mean Mary Ann for the next dance. And the next and the next."

"Oh, darn—"

"It's okay," Lydia said, trying to sound chipper, but not succeeding. "I've decided that come July—that's in five days—I'll have him completely out of my system and be able to concentrate on my future life as a nun. And you, Yoli"—she turned to me like she was cross-examining me—"what's with Benjamín?"

I told her we'd had a nice talk at the party and then met yesterday at the bus stop bench for a little chat. No big deal.

"Oh, wow," she said. She studied me as if she were a detective and I was the suspect.

"He'll be gone the whole month of July," I said. "Like you, I'll probably have him out of my system by the time he gets back. You know the saying, out of sight, out of mind."

"Yeah, sure," Lydia said, looking out on Conifer Street.

And then she suddenly remembered she had house chores to do. "See you later, alligator," she said as she quickly climbed down the tree.

"After a while, crocodile," I called to her. But she didn't even crack a smile.

• • •

On the Fourth of July, American flags fluttered from porches and fences up and down our street. In the distance I noticed Don Epifranio shuffling toward his front fence to his flag holder. He had a cane in one hand and a flag in the other. He was the oldest man on our street—maybe the oldest in San Diego—and the flag he was carrying was as large as he was and probably heavier. It was late to be putting it out—everyone else had had theirs up for days—but he seemed determined to do it anyway. It whipped this way and that in the strong breeze, at times covering his face. Any minute the poor viejito and his flag were going to take flight.

I started running, grateful that I'd won the hundred-yard dash last year.

"Don Epifranio," I called as loudly as I could. He was hard of hearing. "Wait!"

He turned toward my voice. I caught up with him before he could stumble—flag and all.

"Let me help you," I said, taking the flag from him with one hand, steadying him with the other. He squinted at me, trying to bring me into focus.

"I'm Yolanda," I said in a loud voice. "One of the Sahagúns."

He leaned close to me. "Ah, sí, sí. The big brood. What number are you?" he asked.

"I'm number seven," I said.

"For the life of me, I can never remember your names," he said, chuckling. "Pues, you could start—what is it your father says?—a baseball team? Yes, that's it." He nodded. "Un buen equipo de beisbolistas, eh?"

I set the flag on its holder.

He nodded. "Gracias, mi'ja." Then he motioned with his hand

for me to follow and sit with him on his front porch. I helped him up the three steps, and he thanked me as he settled onto his porch chair.

"Your brothers?" he added. "What's going on with them? Will there be any soldier boys in your family?"

I could hear the clanging of metal as barbecue grills were fired up, the neighbors getting ready to grill hot dogs, hamburgers, carne asada, onions, and chiles jalapeños. Someone called out a child's name as a dog barked in the distance.

"Do *you* want my brothers to be soldier boys?" I asked.

He didn't answer immediately. We stared down the street, listening to the freeway whoosh.

"I may be a frail old man, but I'm not an idiot. No," he said, shaking his head. "Let the damn politicians fight their own mess."

"Do you have any ideas on how my brothers—well, Chuy—can avoid being drafted?" I asked him.

"Have you asked Socorrito? She might have some ideas. She's probably a secret comunista," he said, laughing. "But the good kind," he added.

• • •

Socorrito was trimming her hedge, the large garden shears snipping the bush into shape. "Change is coming," was the first thing out of her mouth when I went up to her on my way home from Don Epifranio's. It was as if she was expecting me. "I can feel it in my bones, Yoli."

"Is it good change?" I asked.

"Maybe some good, maybe some bad," she answered.

"What are the good changes?" I was hoping she'd have a lot of good changes to share, but afraid she'd have more bad than good ones.

"Well, for one thing," she said, "we have a new Supreme Court justice. He's Black, and it's about time, is what I say."

I didn't really know what it meant to be a Supreme Court justice, but now was not the time to ask since Socorrito had a habit of taking off on one subject after another as if she were trying to figure out what conversation road she should follow.

"Can you tell me why we're even fighting in this war?" I asked.

"It's complicated, Yoli, like all wars," she said as she continued clipping the bush. "But here's a simple version: There are two Vietnams, north and south, with different government systems. And North Vietnam, led by the Communists, wants to take over South Vietnam, and we don't want them to. So we are helping the South Vietnamese fight them."

Then Socorrito stopped her clipping for a second. "You're worried about Chuy and the war, qué no?"

I nodded, then said, "He's thinking about applying for conscientious objector status, but what can we do if that doesn't keep him from being drafted?"

She looked at me before taking up the garden shears again.

"Pues, I don't know, Yoli," she said, shaking her head and moving to the next shrub. "I don't know."

For the first time since I could remember, Socorrito didn't have long, involved explanations and ready solutions on matters of our country and our world. And for the first time since I could remember, I wished she did.

• • •

A couple of days later I went to the canyon to write in my diary. Sitting on the wooden steps, I could hear a radio playing in the distance, the song about going to San Francisco and wearing flowers in your hair. I set my elbows on my knees and rested my head on my hands, surveying the canyon. What kinds of flowers would I wear? I'd want it to be something growing in my canyon. The yellow sour grass blooms? Maybe a few pink peppercorn sprigs pinned behind my ears and a crown of eucalyptus leaves?

I opened my diary: *July 6, 1967. I wonder what San Francisco is like. Is it really full of hippies and war protesters? If I were to go, I'd be a flower child. I don't know if flower children hop on cable cars, but I would. And I'd lean out the window, waving, and loudly singing my favorite* Sound of Music *songs for all to hear. People walking on the street would hear me sing and join in.*

A jet from the nearby naval station roared above, lighting its afterburners as if it were preparing to drop a bomb. Neighborhood dogs began howling as they did every time the jets shot across the sky over our houses. There'd been a lot of flights this summer, one jet right after the other—three, four, five most days—as if they were in some kind of sky race. *Probably F4 Phantoms,* Tony had once explained, *practicing maneuvers before heading out.*

Heading out to—well, we all knew where. And that sick feeling crept in again.

Before shutting my diary, I wrote: *I pray for this war to be over soon.*

As I made my way up out of the canyon, I wondered if there were ravines like this in Vietnam. What kind of plants and flowers did they have? Walter Cronkite, our favorite TV news anchor, described thick jungles and torrents of rain.

I put my diary away in its box in the toolshed and walked into the house. Most of my family were sitting in front of the TV watching something. Papá was at work and Luz and Monica were at a friend's house down the street.

"...greatest civil rights leaders of America," the man was saying as he introduced the next guest.

I figured the guest must be someone important to have everyone gathered in the sweltering living room on a hot July day. I scooted to the floor and watched, too.

I immediately recognized the name of the man being introduced. Miss Toscano had told us about him, the one who'd given a speech about ending the war. Now I could put a face to the name—Dr. Martin Luther King Jr.—and I liked his face immediately.

It was a kind face, a serious face. He talked slowly and carefully, like Miss Toscano did whenever she had to explain a tricky math problem to the class. Dr. King seemed a little sad, too.

The interviewer asked him about civil rights and nonviolence, and Dr. King explained his stance. During the commercial break, I ran to the bedroom and got my notebook and a pen. When the show returned, I paid close attention, struggling to keep up with him as I jotted down words that seemed important as he talked about the Vietnam War.

Costly. Bloody. Futile. Unjust war.

My hand and pen raced across the paper as my brothers and sisters remained transfixed. Even Tía Matilde and Mamá, from the serious looks on their faces, knew this was an important man with an important message.

When the program came to an end, I glanced at my older siblings—Carolina and Ana, and then at Armando, Octavio, Chuy, and Tony—the way they listened to Dr. King as if their futures depended on it.

• • •

When the phone rang the next Saturday, I picked it up. "Sahagún residence," I said. "Upstairs maid speaking."

I should've guessed who the call was for.

"One moment, please," I said. I placed the handset against my chest so the caller couldn't hear me. "Hey, lover boy," I whispered to Octavio. "It's for you—*again!*"

Octavio and Tony were sitting on the living room floor, surrounded by LPs. Octavio got up and stepped carefully over the records as he took the phone, wiggling his eyebrows at me.

Tony caught my eye and smiled. "Maybe someday Davy Jones'll call you, Yoli."

I shook my head. Brothers.

Once in the front yard, I decided the shady pepper tree was the spot for this hot July day.

From my perch, I spotted El Chango's truck coming up and stopping in front of the house. He and Chuy got out of the truck and stood talking by the front fence.

Whatever Chuy was saying had El Chango laughing.

I quickly climbed down the tree and darted across the street.

"Whoa, where'd you come from?" El Chango asked.

"The tree," I said.

"We have a little tree monkey here," El Chango said.

Chuy looked at me. "What's up, Yoli, Yoli bo-boli?" he said.

A jet from the naval air station shot across the sky.

"Chuy," I said, "did you decide if you're going to apply for conscientious objector?"

I glanced at El Chango with a look that said, *Help me out, please.*

El Chango didn't say anything. He glanced at Chuy in a way that made me realize they'd already had this conversation.

"I decided I've got to try," Chuy said.

"That's great," I said.

"I just hope it works, Yoli."

He picked up a rock and pitched it toward the empty lot across the street. The three of us watched it land near the pepper tree.

• • •

One evening a few days later I was ironing my assigned pile of laundry in the living room when I overheard Chuy and Armando talking in the kitchen.

"I got the CO application from the Selective Service Office today," Chuy said. "Man, they don't make it easy. I need to get references for the application. Community leaders, that kind of person."

I folded a pressed handkerchief square.

"A priest," Armando said. "A religious leader of our community would impress them and have the most impact on your application."

"I doubt Father Carrasco will give me a reference, but I'll try," Chuy said. "I'll ask my teachers and Mr. Brown, too."

Chuy went out to the patio, and I called to Armando, "Do you think he's going to be approved for CO?"

He came into the living room and said, "I think he's going to have a hard time getting references, what with him having goofed around so much in high school. He probably ticked off a lot of the people he needs to vouch for him. I'm sure Mr. Brown will write one, though."

"What else can he do?"

"I don't think there is anything else he can do. Let's hope I'm wrong about the references and that his application for CO status is accepted."

I looked down at my iron. Oh, shoot! I'd forgotten to prop it up. It sat face down on one of Papá's handkerchiefs. I yanked it up—too late. A brown chevron shape was branded on the handkerchief, and the musty, acrid smell of scorched fabric filled the room.

FOURTEEN

August came, which meant that Armando was leaving to study in Madrid. The Friday night before he was to go, the Browns hosted a bon voyage party for him at their home. They were the family who owned Brown's Market, and Armando had worked for them so long that they were like second parents to him. They'd told him to invite whoever he wanted, and so he told me I could invite Lydia.

Their house sat on a small hill and had a perfect view of Imperial Beach and the ocean. I'd never been here before, though my brothers had learned how to swim in their pool.

Mr. and Mrs. Brown greeted us at the front door, and Papá and Mamá thanked them for hosting their son's party.

"King of the Road" was playing, and the patio was filling up with Armando's friends. Lydia was already there, talking outside with Tony, whom Chuy had dropped off earlier with Armando. Tony had brought over records and was manning the record player. Lydia and I were both dressed in sleeveless cotton blouses and Bermuda shorts with bathing suits underneath, and I was pleased to see, with a quick glance around, that our attire allowed us to blend in with the rest of the partygoers.

Lydia suggested we get in the shallow end, hold on to the side of the pool, and do some leg kicks. "Pretend we're warming up for a big swim."

I shook my head. I was sure we'd look like dorks pretending we knew how to swim. Lucky for us, the pool was crowded, mainly guys splashing and bobbing and playing Marco Polo. We could skip the whole pretending-we-know-how-to-swim charade.

"How about if we just stand here in the middle of the patio," Lydia said, "and check out the cute guys."

I scanned the guests, wondering where Benjamín was right now. He'd been gone all of July with his family in Mexico, and even though it was the second week in August, and he should've been back by now, I hadn't seen him or his family at Mass.

The guest of honor, Armando, was surrounded by his friends, and I overheard lots of joking, warning him to concentrate on his studies. Chuy and Octavio, along with Carolina and Ana, had joined them. Tony, in the meantime, was changing up the music, sometimes playing albums, sometimes selecting singles.

"Johnny Angel" started playing, and if ever there was a song that could cause me pangs of anguish and heartbreak, there it was. I began mouthing the words, having sung them a billion times.

"Are you kidding?" Lydia said. "Don't get all llorona on me, Yoli. Stop it with the weepy, mushy singing already. You're going to make me barf."

"If you barf, it's because of all the cake you probably gorged on before I got here, comelona."

She laughed and said she had to leave already. Her parents were picking her up because they were going to Tijuana early the next morning. "Like I said," she called out, "oh, my sweeeeet Johnny Angel, where are you?" She sang in an awful falsetto voice, making up the words.

My best friend. I waved her away, shaking my head as she stopped to say goodbye to Armando.

I glanced over to where Mamá and Papá were seated—Papá had taken time off from work to be at the party—and Monica and Luz were on their laps. They were chatting with Socorrito and Don Epifranio, and Socorrito was doing most of the yakking, probably about neighborhood gossip and world politics.

I wandered to the farthest end of the yard. From this grand view, I felt as if I were the leader of a country looking down upon her land and her people. Still lights—from offices, homes, and streetlamps—were interspersed with moving ones on cars, trucks, and color-changing traffic signals. Farther west, a sudden, large chunk of darkness. The Pacific Ocean. At night and from this vantage point, it seemed spooky and mysterious. Yet beyond were other countries and cities. How far away was Spain?

I turned my gaze to Conifer Street. Tía Matilde had opted out of the party. She'd started a job as a seamstress at Ratner's on Monday, and by the end of the week, she looked tired. She probably liked having the house to herself on these rare occasions. She read her Bible every night and always had a pen in hand, underlining passages. Once when I asked what her favorite part was, she admitted she was partial to the psalms.

"Why?" I asked her.

"Poetry," she said.

What was Tía Matilde underlining tonight? Given her sad love story, what kind of comfort could she find? If I were in her place, I'd be filled with anger and resentment forever at her parents. If I'd fallen in love with someone like Jeremías, I would've run off with my true love.

What looked like a moving star—an airplane—slowly descended, preparing to land at the San Diego airport. Lights blinking, blinking. And me? Where would I land?

• • •

Armando's flight the next day was scheduled for the evening. We gathered around him as he collected his luggage and waited for Mamá and Papá to take him to the airport. We wouldn't be seeing him until next summer.

Earlier that morning, I had asked Armando if he could recommend a novel about war, something that I might understand.

He looked at me. "Why?" he asked.

"Miss Toscano and Socorrito both said that war is complicated," I said. "And I thought maybe if I read up on war, I'd better understand what they meant by *complicated*."

He motioned for me to follow him. We walked out the back door, through the patio, to the guys' room. He checked the stack of books on top of his dresser. *The Red Badge of Courage. The Bridge over the River Kwai. A Farewell to Arms.*

"We did a whole semester on war in literature," he said, pausing in his search. "Wait. I think I've got the perfect book for you." He crouched next to his bed and reached under, pulling out a box filled with more books. He dug around until he found it.

"What's it called?"

"*The Diary of a Young Girl*," he said, handing it to me.

"This is about war?"

"It's about a lot of things, Yoli."

• • •

"When you return are you going to be speaking with a lisp and use *vosotros* on us?" Carolina asked. "Because you better not," she added.

"Make sure you don't fall in love with some Spanish señorita," Octavio said, "and end up flamenco-dancing your way back home."

Armando laughed, hugged each of us. And when he came to Chuy, he said, "Good luck, hermano."

Chuy gave him a sharp military salute. "You bet," he said.

Always live in the positive.

But in this moment, I wanted to hug them and whisk them both off to Spain.

FIFTEEN

As the president of the PCBG, I felt a certain responsibility not only for the members' bike safety on the roads but also for their nourishment. So the next day after church, I packed peanut butter and jelly sandwiches, apples, Red Vines, and plastic pouches filled with tamarindo paste for each of us. Because I wanted this to be Tía's first big bike adventure outside of our Palm City neighborhood, we were going to Imperial Beach, four miles away.

Mamá was watching me as I placed the food items in each of three lunch bags. I glanced at her. Maybe now was as good a time as any to bring it up.

"Mamá," I said carefully, "there's a good chance that Chuy is going to be drafted into the army. You realize that, don't you?"

Silence from her as she reached for a drinking glass.

"I was thinking that we should talk about this and figure out how to get—"

"I don't want to discuss this right now," she broke in quietly.

"So, then, when?" I said, trying to remain calm, knowing she'd say that.

"That's enough, señorita," she said. She held the glass in her hand and looked at it as if she'd forgotten why she'd reached for it.

"But Mamá, Chuy is going to apply for conscientious objector status, and if Father Carrasco writes a letter of recommendation for him, it would help his chances," I said. "It could keep him out of the war. Could you talk to him?"

"Father Carrasco?" she said. "Yoli, do you really think Father Carrasco would help keep Chuy—or anyone, for that matter—out of this war? This is a priest who is always talking about the evils of communism." She shook her head. "I promise you, I'd talk to him if I thought it would make a difference."

And she was gone, just like that. I stared at her empty glass on the counter and wondered what Mamá was feeling. Did she not want to talk about Chuy and the war because she *lived in the positive*, as Miss Toscana had suggested? Or was she thinking that her prayers—our prayers—were going to see us through this? Or had Mamá already accepted Chuy's fate? Was that why she wouldn't even try with Father Carrasco?

• • •

"Feel the freedom!" I encouraged my charges, though maybe it sounded more like a barking command. How could a few minutes this morning in the kitchen have put me in what Carolina called a *pissed-off mood*?

Vowing to myself that I would not let my little talk with Mamá ruin the day, I pointed west. We were pioneers setting off to explore new territory. Lydia, Tía Matilde, and I quickly mounted our bikes and took off in the direction of the beach. Each basket attached to our handlebars held a sack lunch.

"Libertad!" I shouted.

Midway to the beach, we hung a right and bicycled into the Big Bear supermarket parking lot. While they waited outside, I went in to buy us some 7UP.

I zipped over to aisle 12. Quickly scanning the shelves, I suddenly looked up and spotted him talking to his mother. Benjamín.

Don't faint, Yoli, I told myself.

Mrs. Sandoval greeted me first, asking how my parents were. She was happy to know that my grandfather was doing better. Then she left us, telling Benjamín she'd be in the dairy section.

"So it's 7UP?" he said, smiling, as I reached for three bottles.

I was hoping my hands weren't trembling—I was so excited and embarrassed and flustered.

"Dr Pepper's better," he said.

"It has a weird taste," I said. *Not again! Dumb, dumb, dumb.*

"Or else," he said, "peons just can't appreciate its distinctive flavor."

"Of course not, m'lord," I said with a slight curtsy.

He laughed.

Was I sweaty? Was my ponytail okay? Were my bangs behaving and not sticking up?

"How was your vacation with your abuelitos?" I asked.

"Long and boring, to tell you the truth," he said. "We ended up staying almost two extra weeks. I couldn't wait to get back. We got in late last night. That's why I wasn't at Mass today. And you, Yoli, how has your summer been?"

"Kind of the same," I said. "Long and boring." Had I scrubbed away any little whiteheads on my forehead this morning?

"Can we get together soon?" he asked.

"Yes, uh, sure," I said. *Stay calm, Yoli. Stay calm. Don't let on how much you missed him.*

"Would next Sunday be okay with you?"

"Yes," I said, hoping I wasn't nodding too vigorously. "I've got to go now. My aunt and friend are waiting for me in the parking lot. We're riding our bikes over to the beach."

"Oh, wow." He sounded impressed. "That's a good, long ride. Have fun. See you next weekend at church and Brown's Market."

I waved to him and turned to leave, walking down aisle 12, which suddenly seemed filled with floating clouds and hearts, to the cash registers. *Deep breaths, Yoli. Take deep breaths.*

In case Benjamín was looking out the grocery store window, I expertly pushed off and out of the parking lot. I held my head high and straightened my posture. The sun's rays were peeking through the morning fog. Oh, happy day!

"¡Adelante!" I shouted to my two companions, and onward we rode.

Once at the beach, we walked our bikes in the sand and propped them against a wall of rocks. Then we spread our towels.

"What happened at the market that had you coming out with a big smile on your face, all jolly-like?" Lydia asked. Always suspicious, this one.

"Do people need a reason for smiling?"

"No," she said. "*People* don't. Just you. You were so bossy on our ride over here, Your Majesty."

I laughed. "Your Majesty? Wow, so I've earned a place among royalty?"

"Yeah, but don't change the subject, Miss Queen of Conifer Street," Lydia insisted. "What has you in such a joyful mood?"

I could either shrug and not say anything or tell the truth and risk nonstop teasing from Lydia.

"I ran into Benjamín at the market."

"Ha! I knew it!" Lydia said. "Ben-ja-meeeen," she immediately began singing in her screechy voice. "How I love him and shiver and tremble when I see him in church or Big Bear supermarket—" Lydia broke off into a fit of laughter.

"What a treat to have such a star singer as a best friend," I said, shaking my head. "So mature."

"Benjamín?" Tía Matilde asked. "The altar boy, yes?"

"Uh, yes, that one," I said.

Tía suddenly said to me and Lydia, "Shall we go for a little swim?"

"Huh?" Lydia and I looked at each other. Maybe she was joking.

"A swim?" I asked.

She looked at us. "Do you two not know how to swim?" she asked.

We shook our heads no.

"Ah, okay," she said as she stood up and took off her sunflower blouse, then slipped out of her slacks. "I'll have a go at it myself."

Underneath she wore a black one-piece bathing suit. The corset contraption looked about a hundred years old. A bathing suit for serious swimmers. Or ex-nuns.

Lydia and I watched as Tía Matilde sauntered over to the water, first at ankle level, then knees and waist. She plunged forward to meet the oncoming waves. If my aunt had suddenly begun walking on water, I could not have been more stunned.

"Okaaaay," Lydia said. "This is embarrassing. Your ex-nun aunt from a village in Mexico knows how to swim, and we Southern California girls don't?"

I was about to say something about the ironies of life and how people can surprise you when Lydia shouted, "Oh, crap!" and sprang into action as she ran toward the rocks.

A seagull was perched on the edge of one of the bike baskets and had begun pecking at the lunch bag. Lydia shooed it away just in time.

"I may not know how to swim," she called to me above the sound of the waves, "but no dumb bird is going to steal our lunches." And with that she started running along the beach, madly waving her hands this way and that as she shooed seagulls away.

I could see Tía Matilde's ponytailed hair bobbing above the water, her arms alternately stretching before her. How in the world had she learned to swim? And when?

The gray curtain of fog had disappeared, as it seemed to do about this time every afternoon. The sun felt warm on my back. Maybe I could ask Tía to teach me how to swim.

Tía Matilde came out of the water, shaking her hair. She had a smile on her face, and for a minute she looked like some sort of ancient sea goddess who had secrets yet to tell, wisdom yet to share.

She hurried, shivering, to her beach towel and wrapped it around herself.

Lydia was just a speck along the beach line. I wasn't sure she was winning in the seagull wars, but she seemed to be getting her fair share of exercise.

"How did you learn to swim?" I asked.

She looked at me and smiled. "Jeremías," she said as she bent forward and rubbed her wet hair with an end of the towel. "There was this water tank—like a watering hole—where young people went on the hottest days," she said. "Most of us jovencitas didn't know how to swim, of course. And we certainly didn't wear bathing suits. Shorts and a blouse, nothing scandalous or immodest. In fact, we were not allowed to go to the watering hole if boys were there.

So certain days were designated for boys, and others for girls. But Jeremías and I planned it so that I'd get to the tank later in the day, and when the other girls left, he came out of his hiding place and taught me how to swim," she said. "It was four feet deep, but he taught me to dip my head in the water for as long as I could hold my breath and not be afraid." She smiled, staring at the ocean's horizon. "Plus," she said, chuckling, "I wanted him to be proud of me. To see that I could swim just as well as any American girl."

"You sure did love him a lot," I said.

"You'd be surprised, Yoli," she said, "what love for family and friends can inspire you to do."

"Mission accomplished!" Lydia called out, walking toward us, even as I spotted another seagull landing on a rock near our lunches and taking tentative little hops toward our lunch sacks.

I stared at the ocean—somewhere at the other end, a war was going on—and I wondered what I could do to keep my brother safe.

• • •

Later that day, three happy and sunburned PCBG members biked home, and along the way, Lydia and I belted out *our* rendition of *The Sound of Music*'s "My Favorite Things." Tía Matilde laughed as we sang about warm corn tortillas all smothered with butter, Almond Joys and Snickers and frothy Ibarra, and Palm City Bike Gang excursions in summer. I was hoping Mamá could hear us singing, could see that her rude exit from the kitchen this morning had not spoiled my day, was certainly not going to shut me up. If anything, I was determined to raise the subject of Chuy again as soon as I parked my bike.

There was something new going on with me, a change not only in my body but also in my mind. And there was so much to think about these days—about my family, about myself, and about how maybe, just *maybe*, I'd had a change of heart about becoming a nun. Lydia and I had been eight years old when we'd made the pact, and now that I was twelve years old, excuse me if I wasn't quite as certain anymore.

Just before turning onto Conifer Street, Tía Matilde and I waved goodbye to Lydia as she headed back to Harris Street.

When we came to the front fence, all was quiet—no sound of record-player music, TV voices, nothing. That was strange. There was usually some sort of noisy commotion at our house. I glanced at the yard, which was still blooming with daisies, cosmos, and bougainvillea, but the sweet peas had long since died, their vines taken down, and without their wild and unruly blossoms the bare fence looked sad, more lopsided than usual. It was as if the garden's weary calm was one more telltale sign that summer was coming to an end.

"Do you think I will make a good nun?" I asked Tía Matilde.

"I think you'll make a great whatever-you-set-your-mind-to," she said.

"Do you think Mamá will be disappointed if I don't become a nun?"

"It's a mother's dream, Yoli," she said. "Some parents hope their child will grow up to be a doctor or lawyer. Your mother wants a nun or a priest in the family. But you should talk to her about this."

"What if I don't want to be a nun anymore?" I said quickly, just to get it out.

We stood there on the patio, and I wondered if lightning might strike me.

Before Tía Matilda could say anything, Monica burst out the back door. "We got a call from El Grullo. Abuelito is dying, and Mamá is packing to go back," she reported all in one breathless rush. "She's been crying a whole lot."

I tiptoed into the house and over to Mamá and Papá's bedroom, watching my mother from the doorway as she packed. Her back was to me, but I could tell from her sniffles that she *had* been crying a lot. I wanted to talk to her about Chuy, but seeing her like this, I knew now wasn't the right time. Maybe it wasn't fair of me to judge her. Who was I to be bugging her to think another way?

She looked up and over to me.

"Yoli, could you please hand me the cream, Las Tres Caritas, that's on the dresser?" Her voice was hoarse, and her eyes were red and puffy. Had I ever seen Mamá this sad?

A crocheted white doily served as a placemat for her two bottles of Avon perfume samples, a hand mirror with a matching brush and comb, an ashtray filled with bobby pins, a tube of lipstick, and two pairs of earrings. A round peach-colored box of face powder with a design of dandelion-looking cotton puffs was next to a jar of face cream.

The dainty faces of a blonde, a brunette, and a redheaded lady on the label stared at me as I handed her the face cream. It suddenly occurred to me that Mamá was a woman just like anyone else, a woman who wanted a pretty complexion and wore a bit of makeup.

"Did you ever want to be a nun?" I asked her. The question was random, I knew, and when she glanced at me, I sensed it surprised her, too. I wanted to know something—*anything*—new about Mamá. But even as I asked the question, I wondered why I'd never asked before.

She didn't answer right away. She placed the face cream in her cosmetic case.

"Yes," she said quietly. "Your abuelito especially wanted that for me, more than anything else in the world."

"Why didn't you become one?"

She folded a cotton nightgown dotted with tiny blue flowers.

"For many reasons, Yoli," she said.

"Like what?"

She looked up from her packing. "Yoli, we'll talk about this later—"

"How old were you when you changed your mind?"

She sighed. "About fourteen."

"And what did Abuelito say to you when you didn't want to become one, when you, uh, changed your mind?"

"He didn't say anything," she said. "He didn't talk to me for over a week." Then she started weeping, her body shaking, and I could see her as a young woman. I could see me in her.

"I'm sorry about Abuelito," I said. I imagined my mother dressed in a nun's habit, realizing that if she *had* become a nun, I wouldn't exist.

Mamá stopped what she was doing and came over to hug me for a long time without saying anything, because soon she'd be a daughter again, learning to say goodbye to her papi.

SIXTEEN

School was starting in a few weeks, and I figured Ana, headed to high school, and Carolina, headed to college, would be the best people to give me advice on what to expect as I entered junior high. I just didn't realize their advice would come with so many warnings!

Tip number one: Watch out for your hemlines and Mrs. Bilben, the vice principal.

"I know you're going to roll your skirt up as soon as you leave the house," Carolina said. "Our parents are stricter about hemlines than Mrs. Bilben is, but she's scarier."

"Yeah," said Ana. "She walks around with a ruler and measures suspicious hemlines on dresses and skirts—only allows two inches above the knees. Anything more than that, and you're sent to her office until someone can pick you up and take you home."

Rolled skirts, hemlines, rulers—what were they talking about?

"You'll see, hermanita," said Ana. "It's different from elementary school."

Tip number two: Be nice to everyone, and try not to hang

around with little groups of kids who don't let others join in. *Cliques*, they're called.

"Hard to avoid," Carolina said. "But be nice to all, and try not to be a snob."

"I'm not a snob," I said.

She looked at me.

"I'm not, am I?"

Carolina glanced at the clock. "We're going over to Esther's house," she said. "But we'll give you more tips tomorrow."

"What about PE and showering and all that?" I asked.

Carolina and Ana looked at each other and smiled. "You've got time before school starts, Yoli," Carolina said. "Hold your horses and don't be impatient."

As I watched my sisters walk down the street to their friend's house, I wondered if people saw me as a snob.

I rang up Lydia.

"Am I a snob?" I asked as soon as she answered her telephone.

"Huh?" she asked.

"Do I show off my knowledge or act like I'm better than anyone else?" I said.

"You're you," she said.

"What's *that* supposed to mean?"

"It means I'm dying for a Popsicle," she said. "I'll meet you at Brown's Market, and we can ponder the whole snob thing."

• • •

"You know," she said as we walked out of Brown's Market with our Popsicles, "it's not that you're a snob, Yoli. It's just that you're sort of weird."

"Do I make others feel less than me?"

"No," she said. "I don't want your head to get too big or anything but you were kind of popular in Miss Toscano's class. You're dorky and unaware in a funny way." She chuckled. "I bet you didn't even notice that everyone kind of admired you, tonta."

"Really?" I said. "They did?"

"See?" she said. "Sometimes you *are* a little bit too much in the clouds, Yoli."

We turned onto Conifer Street and headed for our tree.

Popular. Admired. Wow. What was junior high going to be like? Thank heaven for best friends like Lydia to help me understand myself.

• • •

The next day, true to their word, Ana and Carolina continued to give me advice about life in junior high.

Tip number three: Do well in all your classes, but don't kissy up to your teachers—unless you want to be made fun of and hated by all the students at Southwest Junior High.

"When are we going to get to gym class?" I asked. How could my sisters not see that this was the big one, the one that had me crazy worried? To be naked in front of a bunch of strangers! And what about when I had my period?

"Go up to the towel monitor and tell her it's p-day," Ana said. "She'll give you a towel for a sponge bath, and while the others are in the shower stalls, you wipe down your neck and armpits, then hurry up and change into your clothes."

"Could I just be on p-day all year long?"

"The towel monitor writes down your name and the date," Carolina said. "So probably you have to stick to being honest."

But undressing and showering in a locker room full of girls?

"You get used to it," Ana said.

"Think of it this way," said Carolina. "The other girls are probably just as self-conscious as you and will be busy hurrying to change into their regular clothes."

Ana added there'd be one or two girls prancing around like fashion models, showing off their naked bodies and taking their time getting dressed. "Just ignore them," she said. "Let these libertinas steal the show all they want."

And then tip number four.

"Even though you're planning to become a nun," Carolina said, "you're probably going to have crushes on a lot of boys, besides Altar Boy." She warned me that there'd be all kinds of boys—cute, ugly, in-between, pachucos, surfers, and dorks. "Any one of these types can have a crush on *you*, but be careful. Watch out for the bad boys."

"Which ones are the bad boys?" I asked. Was Benjamín one of them? If my anxiety was already high before I talked to my sisters, it had now skyrocketed.

"Go with your gut," Ana said.

"Your intuition," Carolina said, as if that were any clearer. It wasn't.

Maybe it'd been a bad idea to ask my sisters for advice. I should've just gone blindly into seventh grade and tried to figure it out for myself.

Then it occurred to me that my brothers might have some words of wisdom on the matter. Maybe they could point out who the bad boys were.

Armando didn't have to be home for me to know what he'd say—bad boys are the ones who don't study and who get bad grades.

Octavio was just getting off the phone from talking with probably one of his many girlfriends. His advice: "Anyone who reminds you of me—stay away from him, hermanita. Nothing but danger." With a wink.

Even though Tony was just sixteen and had little experience with girls, it seemed only fair to ask him, too. He was cleaning a record album, carefully circling a felt brush around it. "If he's a big fan of Ray Charles, the Rolling Stones, and Jefferson Airplane, then he's all right. If he likes the Monkees—especially that little Davy Jones guy—run the other way."

"Oh, you're so funny," I said, walking away.

Chuy was outside, checking the tires on all our bicycles, making sure they had enough air in them. "First of all," he said, "is he polite and respectful? Does he listen to you? Does the advice he gives you about schoolwork and friends help make you a better person?"

I nodded. That sounded wise.

"Don't forget to let him know, right off the bat, that you have four older brothers who are—"

"Yes, yes, I know," I said, smiling. "Who are strong and very protective of their little sisters."

"Yup," he said. "That's what you need to tell him."

SEVENTEEN

"Are you nervous about starting junior high?" Benjamín asked me Sunday right after handing me my green bottle of 7UP. We were sitting on the bus stop bench, our bikes leaning against the back.

"Yes, kind of," I said. "There'll be kids from other elementary schools going, so it's going to be a lot bigger. I think it'll be like leaving a small town and going to the big city." I didn't want to admit that Carolina and Ana's talk had made me more than a little anxious about starting junior high.

He laughed. "I like that comparison, though I won't know for another year. I stay at Saint Charles up to eighth grade. Then in ninth, I'll be going to Marian High."

"What's it like to be taught by nuns?" I asked. "Are they real strict? Do they hit you on the knuckles with a ruler or spank you with a paddle when you do something wrong?"

Then he really started laughing. "No," he said, shaking his head and taking a drink of his Dr Pepper. "At least not at Saint Charles. Where'd you hear that?"

"I don't know," I said, feeling my face grow warm. What a tonta I was! How could I say such mean things about nuns? I was sure that if Tía Matilde had been a nun teacher, she wouldn't have been rapping students on the knuckles. Where had I heard that version of nuns? In a movie, a story? Or had Papá threatened to send us to Catholic school if we didn't behave and get good grades in public school? Had he warned us that the nuns would spank us?

"Is Father Carrasco the principal of the school?"

He nodded. "Sort of. He's the parish priest, so he's like the leader of Saint Charles. Why do you ask?"

"Just wondering," I said.

• • •

The first day of junior high was just after Labor Day and I was a wreck!

This whole thing about going to different classrooms—first period, second period, and on until sixth period—and having different teachers for each subject (I miss you, Miss Toscano!) was confusing. For homeroom I was in the 300 building, so when the bell rang for the next period, I had to dash to my locker to get my geography textbook, then rush to the 600 building. And for each period it seemed I had a whole new set of classmates—so many students from different elementary schools. I was glad Lydia and I at least had English and PE together.

"I thought it was going to be worse," Lydia said as we walked home from school for the first time as new seventh graders. We each were carrying textbooks and a three-ring binder filled with a hundred pages of college-ruled notebook paper, a pencil case filled with ten pencils, five pens, a fat eraser, and a pack of spearmint gum. We'd left elementary school behind.

"What do you mean?" I asked. "I thought it was hectic and exhausting."

"Oh, you know. The communal shower thing. I'm not exactly Twiggy, I know that," she said, transferring the textbooks and binder to her left arm. "It's a relief to see *everyone* wrapping towels around their bodies in a hurry."

"Yeah," I nodded. "It *is* a relief, that's for sure."

"Hey," she said. "Do you think we'll have to shower in front of the other nuns when we join the convent?"

I didn't say anything. Instead, I bent down to look at a dandelion growing through the train tracks. I pulled it out and began to blow at its whisker-like tendrils. Wasn't I supposed to make a wish?

"I sure hope not," she continued. "Why don't you ask your aunt?"

"What teachers do you like best so far?" I asked.

"Yoli, are you even listening to what I'm saying?"

I tossed the dandelion. "I don't know, Lydia. Why don't you ask her yourself if you're so interested in convent showering."

"Well," she said, "excuse me for living. I thought you might want to know, too."

"You're so dramática, Lydia," I said. "They probably won't even accept us as nuns anyway."

"*I'm* dramática?" she said. "Hold on, Yoli." She stopped and looked at me. "What do you mean they probably won't even accept us?"

I walked on, ignoring her.

"Hey!" she called out, and ran up to me. She caught my arm and made me stop. "What are you saying to me, Yoli?"

"I don't know, Lydia. But right now I'm tired, and it's so darn hot and we still have about a mile more to go. But sure, yeah, I'll ask Tía Matilde how they handled showering in the convent, okay?"

We walked the rest of the way in silence. I could tell Lydia was hurt. When we came to her street, we didn't even say goodbye, and I didn't care. I just wanted to be like the dandelion head, flitting away in the breeze.

Once home, I tossed my school stuff on the couch while calling out, "I'll be in the canyon."

"Hold on." Carolina came into the living room. "Well?" she said. "How was your first day of junior high?"

"It was fine," I said. "Just real hot, the classrooms and all." I was in no mood for chitchat or Dear Abby advice.

"Do you have classes with any of your Bayside Elementary friends? With Lydia?"

"We have two classes together," I said. "I'm thirsty. Can we talk about this later?"

She looked at me, worried. "Was it that awful?"

I suddenly felt bad being snippy to Carolina. She was only

125

trying to be a nice big sister. "When do you start your first day of college?" I asked.

"Not until next week," she said. "That's okay, Yoli. We'll chat later. There's juice in the refrigerator."

The house was quiet, and I assumed Ana was showering, which she liked to schedule in the four o'clock time slot, and I could hear Monica and Luz in the side yard talking to Tía Matilde, who was probably watering the plants. Oh, to be back in elementary school, where things seemed so much simpler.

I gulped down a glass of orange juice and then headed out.

In the few minutes it took me to retrieve my diary and cross the street, I felt myself coming back to life.

I sat on the canyon steps and opened my diary: *September 5, 1967. My first day of junior high and I'm not sure I like it.*

• • •

By the end of the week, I was getting the hang of it, this junior high school life, and Lydia had decided to forgive me my grumpiness. "It has been darn hot," she admitted in PE class as we suited up in our white one-piece gym outfits. "Makes for bad moods, I guess."

Calisthenics: jumping jacks, knee bends, side bends, forward bends—"Come on now, girls, reach for those toes!"—followed by a jog around the track.

"Is she kidding?" I said as we began our unmerciful jog. "How about if we crawl to the finish line?"

"Complain, complain," Lydia said. "Is that your middle name?"

"What are you, my mother? Can't I complain in peace?"

Miss Paluck shouted for us to pick up our pace. "Hup, two, three, four—come on, girls!" she called out to us, cupping her hands around her mouth as a megaphone. Our PE teacher was one of our favorites, even if she did sometimes sound like a drill sergeant.

Our English teacher, on the other hand, was just okay. "Nothing to write home about," Lydia whispered to me as Mrs. Benson went over book report format and passed out a list of recommended books to read. Lydia and I had already read most of them.

Geography with Miss Davis was a whole lot more interesting. She taught us fun things like tricks to memorize countries and capital cities. For our first oral report, we had to choose a country and describe what made it special—what the terrain was like, the climate, and resources, that sort of thing. It was due at the end of October, and she encouraged us to pick countries we knew nothing about. Antonio started to say Mexico, but Miss Davis gave him a look. "Stretch yourself, people!" she called to the class as we studied the world atlas.

I chose Vietnam.

Miss Davis looked up from the sign-up sheet. "North or South, or both?" she asked.

"Both, but mostly South," I said. "Where the war is."

EIGHTEEN

The next week flew by. On Saturday, I realized Chuy's meeting with Father Carrasco was scheduled for the following Friday, six miserable days away, and I felt sick with worry. I couldn't concentrate on my homework, didn't even feel like sitting in the canyon or climbing my tree. It occurred to me that if anyone could understand a priest, it had to be an ex-nun, so I sought out Tía Matilde. She was in the kitchen looking through *The American Woman's Cook Book*, Mamá's favorite. The book was tattered and worn, and Tía Matilde handled the pages as if they were from an ancient Bible.

She was studying a full-color photo of a tray of cheese-and-olive canapés.

"This looks enticing, don't you think?" she said.

I nodded, avoiding her eyes.

"Yoli, are you all right?" she said. "What's wrong?" She gently closed the cookbook and gave me her full attention.

I had been all set to talk to her about Father Carrasco, but I couldn't do it. I wanted her to fill me with hope, but I was afraid she wouldn't be able to.

"I'm okay," I said, putting on a smile. "They look pretty," I said, pointing to the cookbook. "The canapés. Fancy. But why go to all that trouble for something that's going to be eaten in one quick bite?"

She laughed.

I stared out the window trying to figure out how to calm myself down. Maybe weeding the garden would help clear the weeds in my mind.

As soon as I knelt in the flower bed and started pulling up the invaders, Chuy came up to me. "Hey, what's going on, hermanita?"

"What do you mean?" I asked.

"You're pulling on those weeds like they're evil body snatchers," he said. "Junior high tough, Yoli bo-boli?"

"When you made the appointment with Father Carrasco, did you tell him what it was about?" I asked.

"His secretary took the call," he said, kneeling next to me and pulling a weed. "She asked what this was in reference to, and I said it had to do with my moral conscience. Why do you ask?"

"Just wondering," I said.

He tugged at a stubborn stem. "I think I have a strong case to make to Father Carrasco, Yoli," he said. "I really do."

"You're hopeful, Chuy?"

"Yup," he said. "But hey, Yoli," he said. "¿Sabes qué? What's going to happen is going to happen. He'll either write the letter or not. Simple as that. Coach Finnerty and even my grumpy English teacher,

Mrs. Carpenter, agreed to write letters. I wasn't a stellar high school student, but they did have a soft spot for my antics. And Mr. Brown was happy to write a letter, claims Armando and I have been his best workers."

"And there's Father Stadler you could ask, right?"

"The thing is, if Father Carrasco, as the head parish priest, says yes, then I won't need Father Stadler's letter," he said. "And if Father Carrasco says no, I'm pretty sure Father Stadler, as second in command, won't want to make waves with Carrasco, so he'll say no, too. Let's just see how this plays out."

I looked at him, my favorite brother. Was he just pretending to be indifferent, to be letting things unfold as they might?

"But in the end, Yoli," he said, playfully tugging on my ear, "it's gonna be okay. We gotta keep the faith no matter what. ¿No crees, hermanita?"

I nodded, trying to smile.

We soon had a large pile of plucked weeds and withered flowers. I wanted to cry out or scream at the top of my lungs. But that wouldn't have done any good, other than to make me look like a loca.

He'd scooted down toward the other end of the flower bed near the small birdbath. Plenty of weeds there.

"What if it's not okay, Chuy? What if keeping the faith isn't enough?"

He looked at me, straightening into an upright kneeling position and brushing the dirt from his hands. "You're right," he said, sighing. "Maybe it isn't enough." He tried on a smile, like me, but it didn't work. "I don't know the answer to that."

A dove alighted on the edge of the birdbath a couple of feet from Chuy. The soft gray bird cooed and then, as if suddenly aware of our proximity, quickly flitted off with a trembly whistle sound.

• • •

The next day during Mass, I looked over at Benjamín, who was watching me. I gave him the Communion nod. I needed to talk to someone, and he knew Father Carrasco better than I did. Maybe he could give me some reassurance that our parish priest would write the letter of recommendation.

At two o'clock, I biked over to the bus stop at Hollister and Palm Streets.

"Would you like to stop in at Brown's Market?" I asked him first thing.

"Sure," he said. "You want a 7UP?"

"Not right now. My brother Chuy's working there," I said, "and I'd like you to meet him."

Benjamín looked at me, hesitating. "You want his approval of me, is that it?" he said.

I laughed, my face warm with embarrassment. "It's not that," I said. "I'm pretty sure he'll like you and all—"

"I'd be honored, Yoli."

Chuy was at the cash register, ringing up a customer. There

were three other people in line, so the introductions were quick, between customers. They shook hands—"Nice to meet you," "Likewise"—and as Benjamín led us out, I glanced back at Chuy. He grinned at me and winked.

"I can tell you're really close to your brother," Benjamín said. "You seem like a close-knit family."

I nodded.

"Yoli," he said, "you okay?"

I looked at him. He had the longest, most beautiful eyelashes.

"I'm worried," I said. "But it's just...I don't know." How could I explain that I felt both hope and despair? So instead, I said nothing, just stared at the cars driving past on Hollister.

"How about if I get you an Almond Joy or a 7UP or something?" he said.

I smiled at him. "No, thank you."

He looked at me, hesitating. "Yoli, I know I don't know you that well and all, but you know you can talk to me. I'm happy to listen."

"Do you think Father Carrasco will write a letter for Chuy recommending he not be in the war?"

Benjamín shrugged and we both sat down on the bench. "He's a hard one to figure out. One moment he's all grumpy with us altar boys, and the next he's real nice."

"But he always ends his sermons with praying for peace and an end to the war," I said. "I'm hoping he will write the letter."

"I really appreciate the confianza you have in me to share your feelings," Benjamín said. "You should feel good about wanting to protect your brother, and you should stay hopeful."

Neither of us made a move to go, as if there were still some unfinished business to this meeting.

"You're right, Benjamín," I finally said. "I should stay hopeful."

• • •

Later that afternoon an ambulance raced down the freeway, its siren shrill and urgent, making the crow perched on a nearby eucalyptus branch fly away, cawing in apparent agitation. So dramáticos, these birds in my neighborhood. I glanced at my diary balanced on my knees. I should write about my friendship with Lydia, try to figure out why I was pushing her away, but I wasn't in the mood.

I took up my pen: *September 17, 1967. Mrs. Benjamín Sandoval.* Then *Mrs. Yolanda Sahagún Sandoval. Mrs. Y. Sandoval. Mrs. Yolanda Sahagún Ramos de Sandoval.* I wrote with a flourish, adding curlicues to the arms of the *Y* and a little swirly tail at the end of the *L*.

I paused, spotting that silly crow back on its old perch.

If I were *de Sandoval*, would I need the *Mrs.* before it? Wouldn't *de Sandoval* mean I was married? And did the *de* mean I *belonged* to him or was a part of him, or what?

• • •

While my sisters got ready for bed, changing into their pajamas and taking turns in the bathroom, I sat with Tía Matilde in the living room and watched as she worked on another knitting project.

Like a puppeteer, she expertly handled the two needles as if they were dancing with each other, gracefully yoked by the yarn. A waltz? An Austrian folk dance? The Jarabe Tapatío? I could've sat there listening to the rhythmic *clickety-click* all evening.

"Tía," I finally said, "is faith enough?"

She set her needles down and asked, "Enough for what?"

"Enough to get what you wish for?" I said, though as soon as I blurted it out, I realized how selfish it sounded.

She looked at me and then at her knitting project as if maybe the answer were hiding in the knit-purl pattern. We could hear Carolina banging on a door telling Princess Ana to stop hogging up the bathroom.

"No," my aunt finally said. "Faith isn't enough to get what you wish for, Yoli. That's not the reason to have faith."

"So then what *is* the reason?"

"'Faith is confidence in what we hope for,'" she recited, "'and assurance about what we do not see.'"

I shook my head, frustrated. That made no sense to me.

"*You* had faith," I said. "You joined the convent and devoted every moment of your life to prayer, and still Jeremías was killed."

She nodded thoughtfully. It occurred to me that she'd probably had similar thoughts a billion times. "To be honest with you, mi'ja," she said, her voice sad, resigned. "I have no good answer. None whatsoever."

• • •

That night, just for good measure, I prayed the rosary. I wrapped the necklace-like chain of blue beads around my fingers, gently rubbing each as I progressed in prayer to the next. When I finished, I tucked the rosary under my pillow on the couch, sure that God would hear me.

NINETEEN

When Chuy entered the house after his appointment with Father Carrasco, he didn't seem one bit surprised to find all of us sisters standing there, waiting. We held our breath—nervous but hopeful—as if we were waiting for the jury's verdict.

He took a deep breath, sat down, and looked at us.

If I knew nothing else about my favorite brother, I knew what his look meant.

I started to tremble.

"He accused me of using the Catholic religion to get out of a war that should, *must*, be waged and won," Chuy told us. "He looked at me as if I were an idiot, asked me if I didn't realize we were fighting against Communists who were threatening not only Vietnam but also the whole world with their heathen and unholy ways."

"And what did you say?" I asked. Had Chuy argued with the priest, taken a stand, stomped out of his office?

"I didn't say anything," Chuy said. "I listened to him, and then he told me, 'To the devil with your cowardly conscientious objector application,' and brushed me out of the office as if I were an annoying fly."

"Send the application anyway," Carolina said. "You have the other recommendations."

Yes, yes, we all nodded.

"Yeah, I plan to," he said. He sounded sad, miles away. He got up. "I'm going over to El Chango's."

I hurried behind him. "Chuy!" I called out. I needed to know, to make sure he and I were of a mind. "Chuy, you're not going, right? If this doesn't work out, we'll think of something—" I tried breathing steadily. I didn't want him to think I was a crybaby little sister.

"One way or another, it's going to work out, hermanita," he said. "Don't worry about it, okay?"

I watched as he walked away.

I wasn't sure what everyone else was feeling in that moment. I only knew one thing: to the devil with Father Carrasco's help. We had to find a way—*I* had to find a way.

• • •

On your mark, get set, go! The next day, Lydia and I took off from the Conifer Street signpost to the end of the street, both of us sprinting with all our might, wanting to win. We were in training for the school olympics, the hundred-yard dash being our best shot at a blue-and-red ribbon. I made it to the dead end first, smacking the chain-link fence and trying to catch my breath.

"That's the best you've run, Yoli," Lydia called out between heaving breaths as she lagged.

I stared at the cars on the freeway below.

"I bet you're going to win the race," she said.

I kept taking breaths—deep in, deep out.

"Yoli, is something wrong?" Lydia asked. "Are you okay?"

"Remind me never, *ever*," I said between breaths, "to talk to him again or ever go near him, if I can avoid it."

"Who are you talking about?"

"I mean it. From now on, I'm going to ask who the confessor is, and if it's Father Caca, I'm turning around and going home."

"Father *Caca*?" She stared at me.

"Yes, Father Caca!" I shouted.

"Shhh, Yoli, lower your voice," she said, looking around.

"Father Caca, Father Caca, Father Caca!" I yelled as loud as I could, hoping he could hear me over at the rectory on Nineteenth Street. I shouted it to the trees, and the birds, and the cars and trucks. To the airplanes and helicopters and all the neighbors on Conifer and Citrus Streets, and across the tracks on Harris and Twenty-Fourth. Over to Palm Avenue and up Suicide Hill. Loud enough for the entire world to hear.

"Yoli, don't—"

"Father Ca-ca!" I cried in case she hadn't heard me the first five times.

"What's going on with you?" she asked. "And to say that about a priest—"

"Yeah, y ¿qué?" I said. "That's what he is."

"He's a priest, Yoli," she insisted. "And he goes to people's houses and performs the sacrament of extreme unction in Spanish."

I looked at her as if she were the most naïve person I'd ever met. "He does that because he speaks Spanish," I explained, trying to contain my rage. "That's why he was sent to this parish, so he could give sermons in Spanish to all our families, to serve *us*."

"Yeah, I know," she said. "And he does do good, priestly things."

"You know what, Lydia?" I said, ready to scream. "Don't you dare start giving me sermons and trying to make me feel guilty. If he's so gung-ho about fighting the Communists, why doesn't *he* enlist and go to Vietnam, and leave the rest of us alone?"

"Oh," she said. "What happened, Yoli?"

"He refused to write a letter so that Chuy wouldn't have to go to the war. He says Chuy should go."

"But, Yoli," she said, "maybe he's right and there are good reasons to fight."

"Oh, never mind," I said. I didn't want to argue with Lydia, and I didn't want Chuy to go and risk being killed, and that was that. I told Lydia I'd see her later and took off, running home so I could get my diary. Then I sprinted across the street to the canyon. It was time to have a talk with God.

• • •

Should I begin with the sign of the cross, followed by *Bless me, Father, for I have sinned* . . . ? Or should I start with a rosary? Would God even listen to me, for it was with God directly that I was going to speak—not with his son, Jesus Christ, or Mary, or Saint Joseph, or any of the other family saints. Much as I loved them and wanted their help, this wasn't about a tricycle for Christmas or a new diary with a lock. Nor was it about praying for a Ken doll. This was a talk with God about Chuy and the war.

It was a dry, bright blue September day. As I sat on the wooden steps, I felt a stillness in the air, a muted hush of cars on the freeway—as if all waited to hear what I had to say to God.

"God?" I began. My voice was shaky. Already I felt like crying. I took a deep breath and continued. "Diosito," I said, bowing my head and closing my eyes. "Please forgive me."

Would lightning strike me dead *now*? Or would a burning bush appear? I glanced around. Nothing.

"God, I'm sorry that I was horribly disrespectful to Father Carrasco. I know it doesn't matter why I called him a bad name. I know you don't want to hear my reason, however good it might be. I know that, dear God. I'm very, very sorry, Diosito. I really am."

The wind picked up.

"It's an awful sin," I continued, "and I'm ready to atone for it." I'd learned that word—*atone*—in catechism class. "And I'm sorry that I had doubts about becoming a nun."

I waited in case he whispered something in my ear. Maybe a red-tailed hawk would suddenly glide past me into the canyon—a sign that God had heard me. Memorized prayers swirled through my head: *To Thee do we cry, poor banished children of Eve, to Thee do we send up our sighs... And forgive us our trespasses as we forgive those who trespass against us.... Pray for us sinners, now and at the hour of our death.... O my God, I am heartily sorry for having offended Thee....* Were these prayers helping me along or mocking me?

A sudden gust of dry, hot air blew. It occurred to me that these were just words I was *saying*, words that could disappear in the wind. No! I wanted God not only to hear me loud and clear, but also to know in some concrete, permanent way that I meant it. I looked at my diary. That was it, then, what I needed to do so he'd know I really, really meant it: I needed to write it down. Of course! Writing it down—and in my diary—would be the ultimate promise, it would prove to God how sincere I was. A perfect way to seal the pact.

And so I began: *September 23, 1967. I firmly resolve, with the help of Thy grace, to become a nun when I am an adult. I will serve Thee and the poor and the sick.* My hand trembled as I tightly held the pen between my fingers. This was the right thing to do. *All I ask in return, dear God, is that You find a way of keeping Chuy safe and out of the Vietnam war. I ask this through Christ Our Lord, Amen.*

I reread my words out loud and inserted the word *humbly* before *ask this.*

The canyon looked brittle and scratchy, and this made me think about Vietnam, and there it was! The answer, the thing that would convince God to help: I would be a Catholic missionary nun in Vietnam. I imagined myself in the tropical heat dressed in my long habit, with its veil and bandeau, caring for the sick and the dying. Yes, I'd become a nun, and once the war was over—it had to end sometime—I'd go to Vietnam.

A thought poked me: Was I doing the same thing Tía Matilde had done?

No. She had joined the convent to retreat from the world and the people who wouldn't let her marry her true love. If she couldn't have Jeremías, she'd just live behind the convent walls. But my plan was different. I was willing to go down the nun road, not out of revenge or anger or self-punishment, but out of gratitude to God for granting me my wish. And I knew that if I put my mind to it, I *could* be a very good nun. With God's grace, I would happily help the Vietnamese in their struggle to fix their country after the war, knowing that my brother had been kept safe. Amen.

TWENTY

When we got home from church, Mamá called from El Grullo to tell us Abuelito had died. The funeral would be on Wednesday, Papá reported when he got off the phone, and then Mamá would be coming home as soon as possible.

• • •

The evening she walked in, Papá behind her carrying her suitcase, we ran to her and hugged and cried, and hugged some more. Poor Mamita had lost her father, and we'd lost our abuelito. I felt sad for all of us, but I was glad she was home again.

We all gathered in the kitchen, and while the first shift ate, we shared funny memories of abuelito, trying to keep Mamá's spirits up.

When they finished their dinner, nobody was in a rush to move. The rest of us, the second shift, stood leaning comfortably against the refrigerator, the sink, or the stove. There was something about keeping things just as they were, as if a switch in position might disrupt our family life.

"What have you all been up to?" Mamá asked.

"While you were gone," Carolina said suddenly, out of nowhere,

"Chuy asked Father Carrasco if he would write a letter on his behalf for an application for conscientious objector status. If the application is approved, Chuy wouldn't have to go to Vietnam." She glanced at Chuy as if to say, *Sorry, but we have to talk about this*.

Papá looked at Chuy. "Why wasn't I told about this?" he said, wiping his mouth with the napkin and then tossing it on his plate.

"Because this is my problem, Papá. It doesn't matter now anyway," Chuy said with a wave of his hand. "Father Carrasco said I was a coward for not wanting to fight the Commies." He looked at us. "Maybe he's right."

"I could've told you that was what he was going to say," Papá said, pushing his chair back with an awful screech against the vinyl floor. "Pues claro que he's going to think you're a coward!" he shouted.

We all stared at our father, but nobody said anything. Octavio reached for the salad bowl for a second helping, and Tony ran his finger over the peach fuzz on his upper lip.

"Do *you* think Chuy's a coward for not wanting to fight in this war, Papá?" I asked, almost in a whisper, afraid of the answer.

"¡Claro que no!" he said, sounding hurt, as if I shouldn't have had to ask. "What kind of question is that, for God's sake? I don't want my sons going off to war. But if you don't go, they'll put you in jail. There's nothing you can do about it unless this application you're talking about is honored."

"Well, I've already sent in my application with the reference letters from my teachers and Mr. Brown," Chuy said. "We'll see how it goes."

Nobody said anything. I glanced at Mamá and Papá as if they might have an answer or something to move us forward. Make us hopeful.

Mamá shook her head and sighed. "Let's clear the table so the rest can eat."

She turned to Monica and Luz. "I have in that bag over there—"

And before she could finish her sentence, the little ones were dashing to the living room and hunting in her bag.

And then I thought about *The Sound of Music.* Captain von Trapp had been a respected officer in the Austrian Royal Navy before he retired, and yet at the end of the movie, even *he* was being ordered back into service to fight in a war he despised. If it came to that, could we do our own version of what the von Trapps did—just sneak Chuy over the backcountry hills and into Mexico?

Later that evening, we sisters and Tía Matilde gathered around Mamá in the living room. She wanted to hear every little detail of our lives since she'd been gone. Did Carolina get the work-study job at Southwestern College? Had Ana received the raise from Mrs. Kastlunger for her Saturday housecleaning job? How did I like junior high so far? She claimed Monica and Luz were two feet taller.

"And you, Matilde," she asked. "How is Ratner's treating you?"

"I've been working overtime," Tía Matilde said. "And I have my eye on a little one-bedroom apartment over on Woodlawn—"

"What?" we shouted all at once. "Move?"

She smiled and nodded. "It's nearby, just two bus stops away."

I looked to Mamá. I wanted Tía Matilde to stay with us forever.

"You know that you can live with us as long as you like, Matilde," she said.

"Thank you, Dolores," she said. "It has been an honor to be among such well-behaved and—shall I say—*spirited* children."

We all laughed, though I felt an emptiness I couldn't fill. Tía Matilde had become such a part of the family—governess, friend, cool aunt. And now, especially, I'd need her help, I'd need her to convince me that I could—and *would*—make a good nun.

• • •

In the middle of October an official-looking envelope arrived from the government. I followed Carolina and Ana as they approached Chuy when he got home from work. They handed it to him.

He opened it and read its contents. "Darn!" he said. "Bad news, I'm being drafted." He looked up at us. "I had a feeling this was coming. I'd heard on the news that a few years ago, there were sixteen thousand American soldiers in Nam. This year it's going to be around half a million. I guess the numbers caught up with me... and it didn't help that my CO application was denied."

"Even with the three letters of recommendation?" Ana asked.

"Yup," Chuy said. "Almost no one gets CO status approved these days."

"What does this letter say?" I asked, trying not to have mean thoughts about Father Carrasco.

"I have to report to the draft induction center," Chuy said.

We looked at him.

"It's where you go for processing and to get a physical exam," he explained. "If they don't find anything wrong, then they get the ball rolling to make a soldier out of me."

"But, Chuy—" we three said at the same time.

"Hold on, let's not get all riled up," he said. "If I have to go, I have to go, y ya."

And that's all he had to say on the subject? What was wrong with this brother of mine?

"Chuy, why don't you marry Donna now?" I asked.

Chuy had bought an engagement ring for Donna for her birthday but hadn't popped the question.

"I need to know what's going to happen to me—a deployment, a tour of duty, that sort of thing—before I ask Donna to marry me. It's the fair thing."

"But if you marry her now, you two can take off to El Grullo," I said, trying not to sound like I was pleading, though I was.

Carolina and Ana looked at me as if maybe it wasn't such a bad idea. Chuy didn't say anything.

"Okay, Yoli," Carolina said. "Continue."

"You can get a job at the preparatoria as an English teacher," I continued. "And on weekends you can help our tías and abuelita with chores around the house." It was a perfect setup.

"That's asking a lot of Donna," Chuy said quietly. "And if we moved to Mexico I could never come back. I'd go to jail for desertion if I returned to the U.S., even for a visit. Besides, this is my country, Yoli," Chuy said quietly. "For better or for worse."

He was right. *This* was our country, and the thought of Chuy living the rest of his life so far away from us made me sad. I thought about how, when I was little, he'd let me tag along whenever he went on a quick shopping errand, plopping down five cents more on the store counter for my piece of Bazooka Joe bubble gum. It was Chuy who had taught me how to ride a bike, and it was Chuy who had let me be the first to test-drive the go-kart he'd built.

"Hermanitas," he said to the three of us, "it's going to be okay, really. Now let me go tell Mamá and call Papá."

And to myself, I thought, *Patience, Yolanda*. I'd made a pact with God, and he worked in mysterious ways.

• • •

While I waited for the miracle to happen, I spent the next two weekends tidying up my oral report on Vietnam. I had read the entry about Vietnam in Miss Davis's class encyclopedia and created a poster-board display, outlining a large diagram of the two countries—North and South Vietnam. With my sixty-four-pack of crayons, I filled in North Vietnam, which was rich in gold, with the color Gold. South Vietnam produced rice, coconut palms, nuts, bamboo, rubber, tobacco, sugarcane, corn, and cotton. I crayoned the south with a palm tree (Sea Green), next to a skinny stalk of corn (Goldenrod) and sugar (Raw Umber), with a Periwinkle background. As a finishing touch, I glued on real rice and corn kernels so that they dotted all of South Vietnam.

"Whoa, not too shabby!" Octavio and Chuy startled me from behind.

I felt my face grow warm. I hadn't wanted anyone to know I was doing my report on Vietnam. I'd taken this Saturday afternoon to finish the board because everyone was out.

"Why Vietnam?" Octavio asked.

I shot a glance at Chuy, who studied my board without saying anything.

"I, uh, that was the one..." I couldn't get the words out. "My teacher assigned the countries to us."

Octavio nodded and headed out the back door while Chuy moved closer to the board for a better look at the details. "You did a real good job on this, Yoli," he said. "Nice touch with the rice and corn," he said, tapping the glued kernels. "It looks like a very interesting country, full of beautiful things to see."

"Chuy—" I began.

He quickly shook his head and said, "It's going to be okay. There's a big world out there, and while Armando's in Europe, I'm going to explore the other end, and then I'm going to come back safe and sound and tell you all about it."

He tried on a smile, but it did no good. I didn't feel any better.

He tugged on my pigtail, and as he walked away, he called out, "Your report's going to get an A plus, hermanita!"

TWENTY-ONE

Even before class began, I had a bad feeling about this day. As I walked to geography with my board and index cards, something told me this oral presentation might not go so well.

"My mother wants me to be Dorothy for Halloween, but I told her I'd rather drop dead," Mean Mary Ann was telling someone as I entered the classroom. "I told her I wanted to be the Wicked Witch of the West."

Two others were arguing about who was scarier, the Frankenstein monster or Dracula.

Skeletons, doctors, nurses, ghosts, and Mr. Spock—the way the class was yakking nonstop about costumes, you'd think they were competing for a prize. There was no way I was going to be able to get them to pay attention to my report the day before Halloween.

I looked around at the desks and realized I was the only one who had gone to the trouble of making a presentation board. Feeling like the dorkus maximus that I was, I set it against the chalkboard next to a couple of sticks of white chalk and the black felt eraser, wishing I could erase the whole presentation with one good swipe. It didn't help when Miss Davis pointed to my presentation board. "Now, *this* is how you do a proper oral presentation!" she proclaimed, looking at the other students with a pointed stare.

Now, *this* was how my classmates were going to hate me.

I stood next to my board with its colorful map of North and South Vietnam, and I faced the thirty or so students—Mean Mary Ann, Suzy of the Beautiful House, Dorky Alan, and Cute New Boy Renato among them. Too bad Lydia wasn't in my class. I could've counted on her, at least, to cheer me on with an encouraging smile.

And I began.

"A little louder, Yolanda," Miss Davis said as I squeaked out a first sentence about South Vietnam.

I referred now and then to my index cards: the land, climate, and resources; the people and their work; the mountains and heavy forests making the building of railways difficult, the rivers as important highways.

Miss Davis was seated near the front, so she didn't notice Mean Mary Ann in the last row covering her mouth with a wide pretend yawn, nor did she catch Emilio grinning at me like the devil himself as he kept rubbing the bridge of his nose with his middle finger as a pointer. I tried to ignore them, but soon other students were shifting in their chairs and doodling in their notebooks. I made out the drawing of a pumpkin with drops of blood dripping from its triangle eyes, another person was finishing up a witch with a pointy hat on a broom and her creepy cat with fur sticking up like some mutant porcupine.

Nobody seemed interested in anything I was saying. So I switched gears. "I drew North Vietnam in gold," I said, "because its hills are rich in gold and other min—"

"Why don't you talk about the war and the Commies?" Alan called out to me.

"Yeah," someone else said. "Tell us about the bombs and dead bodies. My dad said a whole bunch of our soldiers are being slaughtered by the Commies."

"Talk about the gooks," another piped in.

"What are *gooks*?" Suzy asked, giggling.

"Quiet!" Miss Davis said, standing up and facing the class. Her face was flushed with annoyance. "That's enough. Let her finish her report." She turned to me. "Continue, Yolanda."

But I didn't.

I stared at them—at the five rows of six desks, each filled with classmates who were only interested in the blood and guts of the Vietnam War.

Then my attention veered to all the maps in the room. There were plenty, and these did not even include the rolled-up ones hanging from the chalkboard. Whenever Miss Davis wanted to focus on a particular mountain range, river, gulf, ocean, or sea, she pulled down a map as if it were a window blind and pointed to the topography in question. Tacked to the side bulletin board was a map of Europe, and next to it one of Africa. The third showcased the Middle East and, to the north, a huge land mass labeled

USSR. To the southeast of this large country was a plump People's Republic of China, and below it dangled the tiny linked countries of Indochina. These squiggly, smaller ones were lost in the busyness of so many other little countries and islands. And though I had to squint to locate it, I spotted Vietnam.

"Yolanda?"

The classroom also had three globes, each atop a file cabinet. I thought how when you spun the globe, you'd close your eyes and let your finger land on a spot. That'd be your next travel destination, and it would naturally be a country free of war.

It was Emilio who did it, slouched in his seat at the back of the room where only I could see him. He took his pointer finger and thumb and aimed at me as if he had a gun. *Click* went his thumb. And though it was only a joke, a stupid thing guys did, I felt as if a sniper had found my brother and shot and killed him—and now Chuy was lying sprawled in a rice paddy, far away from me and my family. Alone and dead.

"Yolanda, are you all right?" Miss Davis said, and I could hear her loud and clear, but I didn't care that she and every one of my classmates—especially Mean Mary Ann and Alan and Renato, the cute guy—were staring at me, silent, as if they were alert to some dramatic moment about to happen.

I left my presentation board on the chalkboard tray, walked to my desk, and reached for my purse hanging on the back of my seat. I slung its strap over my shoulder and headed to the door. Miss

Davis called out to me. I wasn't sure what she was saying, but it didn't matter—all jibber-jabber tonterías.

I quietly closed the door behind me.

Once in the hallway, I kept up a good, strong pace down the 600 building corridor, heading toward the lunch compound that was eerily empty that time of day. The school offices were at the other end of the grounds, as if the principal and counselors and secretaries wanted to be as far away from us teenagers as possible.

I left all that behind. The grassy slope leading to the street gave a soft, cushy step to my walk, and once on Iris Avenue, I quickened my pace—first a slow jog, then faster and faster still—until I spotted the train tracks that would lead me home.

TWENTY-TWO

"Thanks," Lydia said as we swapped Baby Ruths for Almond Joys. I wasn't a big fan of Baby Ruths, and Lydia could do without what she referred to as *so much coconutty joy*.

"Did we get any Dracula teeth?" I asked. "I thought Don Epifranio gave those out every year, but I can't find mine. Oh, here they are."

We were in our tree, sitting cross-legged on the piece of plywood. Our bags of Halloween candy were on our laps, but this year's loot wasn't that hefty. Yesterday, I had told Lydia—who was decked out in a colorful clown costume, while I was wearing just a dumb pointy witch hat, a black blouse, and slacks—that I just wanted to trick-or-treat on Conifer, Citrus, and Harris. We usually did five or six blocks plus a long stretch of Hollister. She'd looked at me and nodded. I was relieved that she didn't ask why.

"Hey!" somebody called to us from below.

"Quick!" Lydia whispered. "It's Georgie. Put on your red lips."

We each grabbed a pair of waxed candy lips, inserting them into our mouths as if they were retainers.

"You guys want to do some trading?" he shouted. Next to him, Lobo was wagging his tale.

We pointed to our luscious red lips to let him know we couldn't talk, and shook our heads no.

"I have three packs of candy cigarettes," he said.

Georgie did his trick-or-treating in his cousin's neighborhood, Otay, so his stash was different.

Lydia removed her lips. "Really?" she called down to him. "I have Dracula teeth, and you can have them if you give me a pack of cigarettes."

I started laughing.

"Gonna get it out of my system now," she whispered to me with a wink. "This way I won't have the urge to smoke real cigarettes. Once we're nuns, there's going to be a lot of things we'll have to sacrifice. Probably including candy cigarettes."

She tossed Georgie a pack of Dracula teeth, and so did I. Then he climbed halfway up the tree, and we reached down as he handed us each a pack of the chalky candy.

"Hey, thanks," he said, unwrapping the teeth and quickly adjusting them over his own.

We nodded appreciatively at his new fangs. Scary enough.

He pedaled away, Lobo trotting at his side.

"What happened Monday?" Lydia suddenly asked.

I looked at her.

"In your geography class," she said. "When you weren't in PE, I asked Suzy where you were, and she said you'd left class in the middle of your presentation."

I studied my pack of candy cigarettes.

"It's okay if you don't want to talk about it, Yoli," she said. "I didn't ask you about it yesterday because you seemed so upset and I didn't want to make it worse. Does it have to do with the stuff going on with Chuy? Your presentation was on Vietnam. Was that what made you feel, I don't know, sad or something?"

"Yeah," I said, nodding. "But I kind of still don't want to talk about it. Here, you can have these." I handed her my pack of cigarettes.

"So, um, has your geography class started with the states yet?" Lydia asked, taking them.

I shook my head no.

Her third-period geography class with Miss Davis was ahead of mine. They'd all presented their countries and were now focusing on the United States.

"I picked Pennsylvania," she said. "Make sure you do, too."

I sorted through my bag.

"Miss Davis wants us to build a shoebox diorama," she said. "Hey, how about if I ask her if we can do it together? I'll explain that we're planning to join Our Lady of Angels in Pennsylvania."

I was thinking about Vietnam and where Chuy would be in its tropical jungles and the malaria and dengue fever, and how later when I was a nun, I'd be caring for the sick after the war. I hadn't yet told Lydia my new plan. Once she knew it, she'd be angry. This much I was sure of.

"Sure, go ahead and ask Miss Davis," I said.

• • •

I hadn't seen Benjamín outside of church since I had made my pact with God. When he asked to get together, I told him I was busy with family. But now it was the first Sunday in November, and I thought this was as good a time as ever to do it before I lost my nerve and before December rolled around. Because once we were in December there'd be the novena in honor of Our Lady of Guadalupe—nine days of rosaries followed by a Mass and the party on the last day. I'd see him there. Better to get it over with now.

When I went up to the altar to receive Communion, I made eye contact with him and gave him a slight nod. Bus stop today at two o'clock. He gave a slight nod back.

• • •

The air was warm and dry, and the Santa Ana desert winds were stirring. Under other circumstances, I would have loved that the weather was cooperating with my hair, keeping it straight and smooth, but now what did it matter? Who was I trying to impress? What I was about to do would be a big sacrifice as part of my pact with God.

As I pedaled my bike to our designated meeting spot, I thought about how I was going to tell Benjamín.

In the distance, he waved to me with his great Frankie Avalon smile, and I had to admit that my heart did at least two bumbling cartwheels.

"You probably have a pile of these," he said when I rode up. "But here are a few more to add to your stash." He handed me five Almond Joys.

The old Yoli would have thought, *I'll keep these forever and ever, and never unwrap them because they have Benjamín's fingerprints on them. And I'll place the five pieces of candy in my hope chest, which I don't have yet, but will get so I can put these in it—a precious token of his affection for me.*

"Thank you," I said politely, taking the candy bars and stuffing them in the pocket of my knee-length Bermuda shorts. "The reason I asked that we get together today," I barreled on, "is to let you know that I can't meet up with you anymore." I said it in one hurried breath before I lost my nerve.

He looked at me funny, as if I were talking a language he didn't know.

"Did I hurt your feelings in some way, Yoli?"

This was harder than I thought it would be. He was sincere and cute, and—who knows—maybe I really would've wanted to marry him when I was old enough. And we might have made a great couple—Mrs. Yolanda Sandoval, wife of Benjamín Sandoval. But that future was no longer. I had faith that if I stuck to my end of the bargain, God would grant me my request. And since I couldn't immediately join the convent, I had to demonstrate to God that I was seriously on that path. This show of purpose included saying goodbye to any guy I was interested in now and in the future. My brother's life was depending on it.

I shook my head. I was determined to pass God's test. "I just can't," I said. "I'm sorry."

"We can't be *friends*?" He looked at me in a way that made me want to suddenly hug him and tell him I was just kidding. Was his heart breaking like mine?

"No," I said. "No, we can't."

I turned my bike around to leave before I said something stupid, like *Not really, ha-ha, I was just kidding!*

"Yoli," he said. "What is it? What's changed?"

I paused, wanting to say something, soften this goodbye—soften it for him and for me.

What's changed? I thought. *The whole world, that's what.*

I gulped to keep from crying.

A city bus pulled up to the stop, and as the door whooshed open, we shook our heads no to the bus driver.

Benjamín looked at me with a look that said, *What's going on?*

"Thank you and goodbye, Benjamín Sandoval." I quickly hopped on my bike and left him behind.

With each pedal push, I could hear the crinkle of the Almond Joy wrappers in my pocket. All the way down Hollister, I blinked to keep the tears from hindering my vision. Lucky for me, there was little traffic on this warm Sunday afternoon in November.

As I turned left onto Conifer Street, a tumbleweed the size of my bike rolled into my path, and I instinctively swerved to keep from colliding with it. That was a close call.

I glanced back and suddenly thought of something. I made a quick U-turn and sped toward it, riding right through the middle of the dried, thorny bush. More proof of my promise to God.

TWENTY-THREE

It was starting to seem like it'd be a miserable November. After my talk with Benjamín, I decided I'd start going with my parents to seven-thirty Mass, knowing that he wouldn't be there.

"Seven-thirty Mass?" Mamá looked at me as if maybe I was sick or something. "You've suddenly become quite the early bird."

No, not really. But I had to do it.

"El que madruga, Dios lo ayuda," was Papá's happy saying as we three climbed into the pickup. I hoped he was right and that this torture of waking up early would encourage God to help me.

Father Stadler gave the Mass, which was a relief. It had been hard to see Father Carrasco at nine o'clock mass, partly because of my secret embarrassment over having called him Father Caca, but also partly because of my anger over his refusal to write the letter for Chuy.

After Mass, Mamá stopped to greet and chat with one of the Guadalupana members. Papá and I headed to his pickup to wait for her.

"Does Father Stadler always give the seven-thirty Mass?" I asked him.

He nodded. "Yes, most of the time," he said. "Why do you ask?"

"You don't mind that he doesn't give it in Spanish, do you?"

"No," he said. "While everyone is reciting the Our Father, I say a quick Padre Nuestro." He looked at me, smiling. "Prayer is prayer in any language, Yoli. And seven-thirty Mass is a more convenient time for me. I have a lot to do around the house before I head back to work."

I nodded. It was true about him having lots of chores to do around the house on the weekend: a clogged sink that needed unclogging (one of us kids as his assistant), the wringer washer not wringing properly, the front-door screen needing to be replaced (again!), and a dozen other jobs he felt only he could handle.

As Mamá made her way to us across the parking lot, I glanced at Papá, feeling proud that he was my papá.

• • •

Later in this depressing month, I knocked on my brothers' bedroom door.

"What?" shouted Tony.

"Is Chuy there?" I called.

Tony opened the door as he was buttoning his shirt.

"He left for work."

"Oh, okay," I said, beginning to retrace my steps.

"Hey, Yoli," he said.

I turned around.

"It might be over soon," he said.

He had the kind of expression that sixteen-year-old brothers seemed to have for their little sisters—something between annoyance and love.

"The war, you know," he said. "It could soon be over."

I looked at him.

He came out of the guys' bedroom room and onto the patio. We made ourselves comfortable on patio chairs. This I had to hear.

"Why do you say that?" I held my breath, afraid to be too hopeful.

"General Westmoreland just announced that the enemy is now losing," he said. "I think the end is near and they'll surrender soon."

"Really?" I asked. I let out a sigh that was partly quivering.

He nodded. "And last month there were a lot of protests against the war," he said, excited. "Thousands of people showed up at the Pentagon."

"Thousands?" My heart was rising, getting ready to sing. "And the songs, Tony? Didn't you say there were lots of songs against the war?"

"Oh, yeah!" he said, as if I'd hit the right chord in *his* heart. "I'll play some for you sometime."

He got up to leave.

"Tony?" I said, looking up at him. "You really think it'll be over soon? Like really, really?"

"Yup, I really do. Cheer up, hermanita, and start smiling more," he said as he used his fingers to playfully lift his mouth into a happy face.

I watched him walk to the front of the house and then out to the street. He seemed to *saunter*—was that the word?—as if he was confident that bad things would not happen to us. Did that mean my pact with God was working?

TWENTY-FOUR

While Carolina and Tía Matilde shopped at Big Bear supermarket for last-minute items needed for our Thanksgiving dinner, the rest of us girls were in the kitchen helping Mamá.

"Can't you try one more time to convince Tía Matilde to stay with us?" I asked. "We've gotten so used to her and love her company."

"Tell her she'd be saving a lot of money living with us," Ana said. She was grating tons of carrots for her famous carrot salad.

Mamá was basting the turkey, brushing it in long, precise strokes as if she were painting the large bird for an art exhibit. She glanced at me as I chopped the celery.

"I *have* told her that," Mamá said. "I've given her many reasons why we would love for her to stay." She opened the oven door and placed the turkey back inside. "But you also need to understand that she might want some privacy."

"Why does she need to have privacy?" Monica asked.

"Won't she be scared to live alone?" Luz asked. She was cradling her doll while pretend-feeding it some granules of sugar. Most of the sugar was falling to the floor.

"Stop that or you're going to attract ants," I told her. "And at night they're going to crawl all over your body, taking little bites out of you and your doll—"

Mamá gave me a look. Then, turning to Luz, she told her to stop making a sugary mess.

Maybe I should move in with Tía Matilde to get away from this house of creepy dolls and annoying little sisters.

"That's enough celery, Yoli."

That way, I went on with my thoughts, Tía Matilde could tutor me on convent life. I'd never tell her or anyone about my pact with God. All she needed to know was that I was now sure I wanted to be a nun, and I needed to prepare to be one.

I chopped faster, the celery chunks thinner.

Who better than this former nun to teach me how to be a devout and supplicant servant of God?

"Yoli, ya basta!" Mamá said, bringing my thoughts back to the kitchen. "I said that's enough. Didn't you hear me the first time?"

I looked down at the chopping board. In my excitement to move in with Tía Matilde, I had created a Mount Everest of chopped celery instead of just one cup. Oops.

Once relieved of my kitchen duties, I made a beeline to my tree across the street. I snipped a few peppercorn twigs and slim leaf branches—stems long enough to fit into small flower vases as table centerpieces.

Back at the house, the smells of Thanksgiving were everywhere. I deeply inhaled the sweet and tangy aromas. Oh, thank you, God!

Every Thanksgiving we borrowed extra tables and metal chairs from Saint Charles's parish hall, and lined the tables up as one long banquet area across the living room and kitchen. As I set the twigs and leaves in small jars along the length of the table, I imagined I was Headmistress of Household Matters at one of the elegant dining halls of Austrian estates—maybe the von Trapps' abode? When you squinted just so, all things were possible.

The front screen door opened with its usual whiny creak. Tía Matilde and Carolina were back from the market. The show was about to begin.

• • •

Bless us, O Lord, and these Thy gifts, which we are about to receive from Thy bounty through Christ our Lord.

"Amen," we said in unison.

Papá stood up, tapping a glass with his fork until we quieted down. "I'm sure I speak for everyone when I say that I am grateful to your tía Matilde for taking care of all of you." Turning to her, he said, "You will be greatly missed, Matilde. Your stay has been a gift for all of us."

"If ever you feel you want to come back and live with us," Mamá added, "you know that this is your home."

The rest of us nodded in agreement.

"Why don't you stay?" little Luz asked. "We can find you privacy here."

We all started laughing.

Luz looked at us, confused.

Carolina, sitting next to her, leaned toward her. "Privacy means…" But then she shook her head and straightened up. "Never mind," she said. "Why bother? The concept is nonexistent in this family anyway."

"This has been a gift for *me*," Tía Matilde said, looking from one to the other of us. "Obedient and charming soldaditos, everyone said. And they were right."

"Speaking of soldiers," Chuy said, looking at our parents, "I've received my orders to report to Fort Ord for basic training on January first."

Just like that. No clearing of the throat, no *ums* and *errs*. It was as if Chuy were mentioning he was swinging by the market, did we need any last-minute items?

"No!" I shouted, pushing the metal chair and standing up. It fell backward on the vinyl floor with a loud, metallic clang. "No, you shouldn't go, Chuy."

"Yolanda Sahagún!" Papá pounded his fists on the table and rose to his feet. "Calm yourself down right this minute."

"That's the problem, don't you see?" I shouted, looking at each of them. "We're so well-behaved, just like a bunch of sheep. *Soldaditos* is sure as heck what we are, and off we march to fight some stupid war." I was crying and couldn't stop. "We should've written to Dr. King. He would've helped prevent Chuy from going to war."

My body felt ready to crumble into a heap of tears and anger. Tía Matilde, sitting next to me, got up and wrapped her arms around me. I pressed my face against her chest, still sobbing. Soon Luz started crying, and then Monica.

Papá continued: "You're too young to understand these things. Yolanda—"

"Too young?" I shouted as I tried to catch my breath. "How old do I have to be to understand that—"

I looked at Chuy and stopped myself. *That my brother could be killed in this war.*

I heard Chuy's voice. "Hey, kiddo," he said, now standing next to us. "It's going to be okay, Yoli bo-boli," he said, patting my back as Tía Matilde continued to hug me. "It's gonna be all right."

Everyone at the table had questions: Why didn't you tell us sooner? Where's Fort Ord? How long is training? When will you be heading to Vietnam? For how long?

"Will everyone be quiet and calm down!" Mamá shouted above the barrage of questions. "Sit down. Cálmense." She glanced at Chuy. "Lorenzo," she said to Papá, "please carve the turkey. After dinner, we'll remove the tables and pray the rosary."

I stared at Mamá, wanting to accuse her, to scold her, to plead with her. She didn't fool me with her pretend calm.

Carolina was about to speak, but Mamá added: "And I don't

want any arguments about this, and no more talking about this subject." Her voice cracked, her green eyes brimming with tears. "Is it understood?"

Because none of us knew what to do with this moment, we did as Mamá instructed. Not a word, not a peep—nothing—as we served ourselves. It was as if we were at a funeral figuring out how to grieve in our own quiet way. I was sorry that Armando was in Spain and not here with us. I missed him. As a college student, he might have said something encouraging and wise.

Green beans, camotes, mashed potatoes with gravy, cranberry compote, mushroom-and-celery stuffing, carrot salad, guacamole, corn tortillas, and Bisquick rolls. Dark meat for some, white meat for others. Pumpkin pie and apple pie, and a dollop of whipped cream. I forced myself to eat, to be grateful for the food before me.

Later, in the quiet of bedtime, I tried to put the afternoon in order, piecing together the parts I understood and having faith in God to piece the ones I couldn't. *God works in mysterious ways. Believe, Yolanda Sahagún*, I repeated in a whisper, in a prayer. *Believe.*

TWENTY-FIVE

*D*ecember 2, 1967. Dear Diary, I pray that I will be the kind of nun to make God and my family very proud. I want to live a life worthy of the promises of Christ and deserving of God's part in our pact.

Sitting on the wooden steps in the canyon, I watched the cars rushing past on Interstate 5. Where were they all going in such a hurry? Where was I going? If my plan was to be a novice at the age of eighteen, would I be able to still apply for my driver's permit at sixteen? Were missionary nuns even allowed to drive? And speaking of driving, I knew there'd be roadblocks and temptations up ahead. Should I steer clear of high school dances? Friday night football games?

Over a week had passed since my *Thanksgiving outburst*, as Carolina called it, and I was still feeling sick just thinking about it all—Chuy being drafted, me feeling desperate to do something, time running out before Chuy left for boot camp. I looked down at my diary. Why bother recording my thoughts and daily routine—what was it for? I'd finished reading *The Diary of a Young Girl*, and I loved it, though I cried at the ending. The awful stuff war does. Still I was no Anne Frank, I wasn't a young girl telling my story of hiding from the Nazis in a secret annex in Europe during World War II. Years from now, who would care what twelve-year-old Yolanda Sahagún of San Diego, California, thought? My writings were merely the silly ramblings of a dramática.

But maybe I needed to write in a diary just for me, to help me figure things out. I opened it and quickly leafed backward through the written pages, until I came to the entry I was looking for. Flourishes and curlicues danced on the page as if the letters were engaged in a waltz one minute, a polka the next. *Mrs. Yolanda Sahagún-Sandoval*—in every imaginable name combination—curtsied, frolicked, and twirled on the page.

I took my pen and with hard, mean strokes, scribbled out the misdirected signatures in my diary, over and over until they were completely blacked out, just a series of thick dark rectangles looking like coffins burying what might've been *Mrs. Benjamín Sandoval.*

• • •

That evening as we sisters and Tía Matilde got ready for bed, I approached Tía Matilde, asking her if I could sleep over at her apartment now and then. (Despite what I'd thought about while chopping celery, I knew Mamá and Papá would never let me go live with her.) She had already paid December's rent and was moving in tomorrow.

Before she could answer, all four sisters popped up out of

nowhere, it seemed—Monica and Luz on the top bunk bed waiting for Ana to read to them, Ana in the bathroom washing her face, and Carolina dressing in her flannel pajamas—and begged to sleep over, too. It seemed we'd all been dying for the chance to have a little bit of privacy now and then, though I couldn't imagine why Monica and Luz were so excited to have their time at Tía Matilde's.

Tía Matilde laughed and said we were *all* invited to come over as often as we wished.

When she took her turn in the bathroom, I whispered my case to my sisters: "I'm preparing to be a nun and need as much guidance from Tía as I can get."

"I'm majoring in psychology," Carolina said, "and I need all the practice I can get. Analyzing former nuns is a perfect place to start."

"And now that she's not a nun, and will be living on her own," Ana pushed in, "she'll need tips on how to apply her makeup so she can catch a man."

We looked at her.

"Well, not that I wear makeup," she said. "But I've been reading magazines that tell you how to do it, once I'm allowed."

We turned to Luz and Monica. What was *their* reason?

"We just want to be with Tía Matilde," they said, looking at each other and shrugging. "Porque sí"—as if *just because* was a good enough reason.

Sisters.

• • •

The next day, Tía Matilde joined Mamá, Papá, and me for early morning Mass, and afterward I got to be the first to help her set up her little nido. I quickly made myself as useful as I could, writing down a list of tasks for me and my sisters, who would be coming later in the afternoon: lining her kitchen cupboards with shelf paper, organizing the flatware and dishes she'd bought at Pic 'N' Save, folding and putting away her sheets and towels.

Now that Tía Matilde had moved out, I had the choice to go back to the girls' bedroom and share a bed with either Ana or Carolina. No, thank you, was my feeling. I liked having my own room even if it was just for overnight.

I made a mental list of the things Tía Matilde could use, figuring we brothers and sisters could pool our money and get her a nice Christmas gift to dress up the apartment. It didn't have to look like a sparse convent cell.

While I measured and cut the shelf paper in the kitchen, I could hear Tía Matilde humming in the bedroom. It didn't sound like any of the songs from the *Sound of Music*, as I might've wished. I stopped what I was doing and listened carefully. She sang softly the Guadalupana song about Juan Dieguito's surprise encounter with the Virgen de Guadalupe in Tepeyac, Mexico. I'd never heard her sing before.

When the singing stopped, I called out to her. "Tía, I'm going to start on the flatware, if that's okay."

She didn't answer, so I went to the bedroom. She was standing near the window, her back to me, and I could see she was holding up a long black robe, as if she was inspecting it for stains. When I took a step closer, I realized it was her nun's habit.

"Oh," she said, turning. "I didn't hear you come in."

"You didn't have to give it back?"

"I asked to keep it," she said. "It was fifteen years of my life."

I didn't say anything. She quickly set it down on the bed.

"May I try it on?" I didn't know if this was a sin or not, trying on someone's else nun habit.

"Pues sí. ¿Por qué no?" she said.

She handed it to me, and I quickly slipped into the gown.

The bedroom door had a full-length mirror, and I stood before it. The hem of the robe swept the floor a good three inches; I had some growing yet to do.

The black fabric felt heavy on my body, as if I were wearing twenty wool coats. Dressed like this in the Vietnamese tropics, I'd be sweating up a storm in no time. In the mirror I avoided looking at my aunt. I tried on a smile—weak, fake—just in case she was watching my reaction. I had hoped putting on the nun's habit would cement my excitement to be a nun, but it didn't.

When I turned around, I realized Tía Matilde had been studying me. I was expecting her to say something like *Oh, how lovely you look, Yolanda! A few adjustments here and there and it will fit you perfectly!*

Nothing.

I sat on the mattress to catch my breath, hoping she didn't notice the tears welling up. "Tía," I asked, my voice hoarse and unsteady, "did you ever regret—" And then I stopped. Of course she regretted it, tonta! She'd already said as much. She should've eloped with Jeremías, instead of becoming a nun.

I supposed what I was really asking was, *Would I regret joining the convent? Would a nun's habit ever fit me quite right?*

"Yoli," she said, putting her arm around my shoulder. "You have a few years ahead of you to decide. This seems to be weighing on you too much, mi'ja." She shook her head. "Don't put that kind of pressure on yourself."

She was right, but I wanted desperately to tell her about my pact with God. Was it okay to bargain with God?

"Are you all right?" she asked. "You seem preocupada. What's wrong?"

"Nothing," I quickly said, trying on a smile.

"Okay." She nodded, not buying my answer, I could tell, but not pushing it. "You've lined all the kitchen cupboards, have you?" she asked. "You're not only a focused worker but an efficient one, too."

I glanced once more at myself in the mirror and then quickly—maybe too quickly?—took off the habit. Because there was something troubling me: What was I going to do if God didn't keep *his* side of the bargain?

• • •

It was warm, windy, and dry later that afternoon, and an invasion of tumbleweed on the streets had Lydia and me rethink going bike riding. I'd finished my tasks at Tía Matilde's, and my sisters had happily hurried over for their turn to help her.

"Where'd all these creepy, mean bushes come from?" she asked. We decided on our tree instead.

"The novena begins tomorrow, you know," Lydia announced. "You'll be seeing your lover boy." She wiggled her eyebrows.

"He's not my lover boy, and I'm not even friends with him anymore."

"Oh, I see," she said. "You got him out of your system?" She squinted at me as if she were trying to look deep into my eyes to find the truth.

"Jeez, is that so hard for you to believe?"

"I wish I could be a witness to how you're going to handle seeing your former love for nine days straight." Lydia's family alternated between Saint Charles and Our Lady of Guadalupe in the nearby neighborhood of Chula Vista. They always celebrated the novena at Our Lady.

I didn't answer. Sometimes Lydia could be a pest, and lucky for me, Mamá had come outside and was calling to me. I had to go home.

The novena would be another test from God, another chance to prove that I was holding up my side of the pact. Benjamín would be there with his family, and there might be a situation where we were within speaking distance. Should I look the other way? Should I ignore him? What if he came up to me and said hello? How would I respond? What if he said he wanted to talk privately with me? And when I politely agreed to a few minutes alone with him, how would I react when he said he missed our friendship?

Or the other, worse option: What if he ignored *me* completely, and didn't give a hoot about me anymore?

• • •

Before dinner, my sisters and I watched the evening news about a surgeon who'd performed the first heart transplant ever, and during dinner we all took turns wondering how he did that, took one heart, and replaced it with another. Whose heart did he use, and would the dead person—the *donor*, Carolina called him—come back to haunt the person who now had his heart? This got us talking about Frankenstein monsters, and soon Monica and Luz were terrified enough not to want to eat the rest of their dinner.

"Ya basta," Mamá said, and that was that.

After dinner, I headed to my brothers' room.

Chuy answered my knock. He was dressed in a light blue shirt and navy-blue slacks.

"You look very handsome, Chuy," I said.

"Going out for some fun before the serious stuff starts," he said.

"With Donna?" I asked.

"Yeah," he said, smiling. "With Donna and El Chango and a few others."

"You leave for boot camp in January, right?" I asked, though we both knew the answer to that.

"I have to go in for some initial processing before Christmas," he said. "Then we get a short Christmas break before the real training begins."

"Are you still going to propose to Donna?" I asked.

"Yeah," he said. "Now that I know the what and when of boot camp and deployment, I'm thinking of proposing Christmas Day."

He playfully tapped my pudgy nose—something he'd always done when I was a little girl—my nose so unlike his slender, perfect one.

"Gotta go," he said.

I watched him leave the patio, head to the car out front. He got in and started the engine.

And what *did* it mean to get a new heart? Did it mean that it would erase the sadness and fear you had in your old one?

TWENTY-SIX

December 4, 1967. It is with the utmost trepidation that I prepare myself for this evening's novena, I wrote in my diary.

Trepidation was one of our new vocabulary words. *Tre-pi-da-tion.* It sounded like the kind of word that warned you to carefully tiptoe in, a word that meant you might trip and fall and make a complete tonta of yourself. Tonight was the first night of the novena to Our Lady of Guadalupe, and I knew I was going to need to *muster* (another new word) as much courage and strength as possible. To meet the evening's rosary without trepidation.

I checked myself one last time in the bedroom mirror—no food between my teeth, no screaming pimples on my face, nothing dangling from my nose. And then an afterthought: What did it matter if my hair looked pretty? Would God care? No. Would Our Lady of Guadalupe nod and smile approvingly? No. Would Saint Charles and Saint Joseph discreetly tip their halos in admiration? No. Then who was I doing it for? I closed my eyes and began reciting in my head the "Juan Dieguito" song—anything to stop thinking of *him.*

We piled into the Rambler, all five girls along with Mamá and

Tía Matilde. Carolina was our chauffeur, since Papá couldn't get away during the week. My brothers, on the other hand, and for reasons that seemed unfair, were not obligated to come to the nine evenings of rosaries. It always seemed they had some good excuse: a lot of homework (Tony), in charge of closing at Brown's Market (Chuy), exhausted from ten-hour shifts at Rohr (Octavio). Really the only one who had a good excuse was Armando, living in Spain.

It bugged Carolina that our brothers got off so easily. It made her *super pissed off*.

We arrived thirty minutes early. As we dipped our fingers in the holy water, crossed ourselves, and quietly walked to our pew, I was finding it hard to breathe. Trepidation was sneaking in.

A few minutes later, Benjamín and his brothers made their arrival known with shuffles, coughs, manly clearing of throats, heavy footsteps, some laughter. If I turned around and looked, I was sure I'd see roughhousing, maybe one of them dipping his fingers in the font and then flicking the water at one of his brothers. Stuff my brothers used to do.

A stealthy glance. They sat three pews behind and across the aisle from us. Good!

This time, neither Carolina nor Ana gave me that look, or the wink-wink because they must've remembered that last week I'd announced that I was "over him."

They'd looked at me and said, "Y ¿eso? What happened?"

"Who knows," I said. "I'm just not interested in him anymore."

"Ahh, puppy love," Carolina had said. "Ever so fickle."

I made it through the twenty-five minutes of Padre Nuestros and Dios Te Salve Marías without glancing over my shoulder. I'd always loved praying the rosary, even if I didn't understand a lot of the litany part—House of Gold? Tower of Ivory? But now, with my pact with God in place, the rosary took on a whole new importance for me—it *had* to.

After Mass, I quickly exited through one of the side doors and was the first to make it to the car, leaving my sisters, Mamá, and Tía Matilde behind to dawdle.

In the eight consecutive days of rosaries, there was no high drama, no accidentally running into him. Everyone sat in the same spot, as if we'd all been assigned a particular pew for the duration of the novena.

• • •

On the ninth and last day, December 12, I dressed in my sixth-grade graduation dress, the one I'd worn the day I talked to Benjamín for the first time in Suzy's rose garden. We were getting *dolled up*, as Carolina called it, for the Guadalupana party after Mass in the parish hall. My shoulder-length light brown hair was behaving beyond my wildest expectations—straight bangs, part in the middle—and as soon as Carolina and Ana cleared out of the bedroom, I quickly snatched Carolina's lipstick and applied a smidgen of Carnation Pink on my lips. What the heck, why not?

Since Mamá insisted Tony join us for Mass that evening, we

had to do a little doubling up in the Rambler: Luz was on my lap, and Monica was on Ana's. Tony was squished between us, while Mamá and Tía Matilde sat up front next to Carolina, our driver. I think Carolina was satisfied that at least one of our brothers was required to come to Mass on the day of Our Lady of Guadalupe. But all it took was one smelly fart from Tony and we wished he *hadn't* come.

As we waited for Mass to begin, I wasn't surprised to see Benjamín, dressed as an altar boy, following Father Carrasco out of the sacristy. I expected as much. Throughout Mass, I stared at the large crucifix affixed to the wall behind the altar or I pretended to be absorbed in reading the missal on my lap—*anything*, as long as my gaze didn't fall on Benjamín.

After the Liturgy of the Word, Father Carrasco stepped up to the pulpit to give his yearly sermon about the Virgen de Guadalupe and how this dark-faced Virgencita chose to appear and make her wishes known to Juan Diego, a humble Mexican peasant.

"We all know the story of the miracle at Tepeyac," Father Carrasco began. But this year he wanted to offer a different story. "Tan esencial," he said, "as the miracle itself."

A few people shifted in their pews, and one gave a shush to a noisy kid. Even I couldn't resist looking up, wondering what this different story would be.

"Had Spanish explorers *not* set foot on Mexican soil in the name of Queen Isabella and in the name of the Roman Catholic Church,

God only knows"—and here Father Carrasco made an exaggerated shudder—"where Mexico and its people would be now."

Silence. It felt like everyone in the church was holding their breath. I thought about my future role as a nun in Vietnam—would the Vietnamese want to be converted? What if they were perfectly happy being Buddhist or following the teachings of Confucius?

"In your prayers," Father Carrasco concluded, "make sure that you pray with enormous gratitude for the Spanish clergy who risked their lives coming to Mexico to convert the illiterate indios." Then he stepped down from the pulpit and walked back to the altar to resume Mass.

There was a kind of quiet I'd never heard in church before, a pause that made me wonder if a bomb was about to explode or a volcano to erupt. Was the San Andreas Fault rumbling into The Big One?

I leaned forward and glanced to the right at Mamá. *Stone-faced* reached new levels. I glanced to my left at Tía Matilde. Her eyes were glistening with held-back tears, and in her face, I detected rage or disgust or—

She stood, stepped out of the pew, walked briskly to the back of the church, and left, slamming the heavy door as hard as she could.

I, too, got up, ready to follow her.

"Don't," Carolina whispered, holding on to my arm. "Mamá's the president," she said. "Stay here to support her."

We got through the rest of Mass, but none of us, not even Mamá, went up to receive Communion. Together we probably had enough mean thoughts to send us straight down to the devil—unless Father Carrasco beat us to hell, in which case our outrage might earn us a place in heaven.

Afterward in the courtyard, the Guadalupana members—all devout Mexican women—gathered around Mamá. She instructed us daughters to go to the car and check on Tía Matilde.

Tía Matilde was leaning against the hood with her arms folded, and when we approached her, she shook her head and simply said, "¡Qué desgraciado!"

So even devout Catholics could disagree with a priest's sermon.

Mamá came to the car and told us all to go to the church hall and help the members set up for the fiesta. She'd be there in a bit.

"Where are you going?" I asked.

"Just go, please," she said.

That was the thing about Mamá. She was a woman of few words, but her face said it all. *Interpret my silence*, she and Papá often said to us when they were not pleased with our behavior. I was now interpreting her silence.

We watched as she headed to the rectory and we to the church hall.

"I hope she gives him crap," Carolina said.

Monica and Luz looked at Carolina. "Why do you say that?" Monica asked. "Did Father Carrasco do something wrong?"

Carolina didn't say anything. We were nearing the parish hall.

"He's a priest," Monica said. "*Can* he do something wrong?"

Carolina abruptly stopped, and we all followed suit. She glanced at Tía Matilde, who shook her head no.

She sighed. "Someday, Monica," Carolina said to our seven-year-old sister, "you're going to discover a world of hypocrisy and injustices. But for now, hermanita, hold on to your world of innocence and purity."

Monica looked at me as if expecting me to translate Carolina's remark.

I shook my head but didn't say anything. *Interpret my silence.*

The hall's ceiling was draped with papel picado—green, white, and red banners of tissue paper in cutout shapes. At the far end, six-foot tables draped with white tablecloths were against the wall, covered with platters of yummy food.

Soon the room filled with the novena congregants, waiting for Father Carrasco. When he entered, dressed in black slacks and his priest shirt and collar, he gave a quick blessing of the food and then excused himself from the party. He seemed to be coming down with something, perhaps the flu, he quickly explained. He didn't want to infect anyone with whatever virus he might have.

"*Infect us* is right," Carolina whispered to Ana and me. "I think he's coming down with *enormous* strains of delusions of grandeur. Him and his fascist beliefs."

I didn't know what *fascist* meant, but judging from Carolina's disgusted tone of voice, it must've meant something bad.

As soon as the priest left the hall, Mamá signaled for the mariachi to begin playing "Las Mañanitas," a salute to Our Lady of Guadalupe. I glanced over at the Sandoval brothers, Benjamín among them, huddled in one corner, eyeing the food and ready to dig in. Benjamín was smiling at something his little brother was saying. I quickly looked away. This was going to be a painful night, I could tell.

"Hey, Yoli," Ana called to me. "They need someone to serve the rice. Go to it."

That was what I was doing when Benjamín came up to me with his plate.

"Hi, Yoli," he said. That Frankie Avalon smile.

"Hi, there," I said as casually as possible as he held out his plate.

My hand was shaking, but I managed to scoop a big spoonful of rice and place it on his plate without dropping a single grain.

"Thank you," he said, and moved to the next server.

The party lasted a couple of hours, and it was for me, as Lydia might say, sweet torture. How I wish she could've been here to keep me on track. She'd know how to distract me with her goofiness. But she wasn't here, and so I was left with this heavy feeling in my heart as I tried not to glance Benjamín's way.

When the mariachi started up with "Sabor a Mi," everyone applauded and stopped what they were doing—eating, chatting, and laughing—and sang along in Spanish.

And I, stupidly and accidentally, looked his way.

Our eyes met.

And it was as if Liesl von Trapp and her beau, Rolf, were in the gazebo singing their love for each other.

Benjamín and I smiled at each other.

And I couldn't deny it any longer: I missed our talks. It'd been so easy to share things with him. He understood my wanting to protect my brother.

Maybe it was just as well Lydia wasn't here. I had to do what my heart seemed to tell me to do.

The opportunity came at the end of the party. Mrs. Sandoval was instructing Benjamín to take empty trays to the kitchen. I looked around. Everyone was busy with a cleanup task. If I didn't do it now, I might not ever. And I'd regret it.

I quickly grabbed my empty tray of rice and headed to the kitchen.

Benjamín was stacking the aluminum trays when I walked in, and his back was to me. Nobody else was in the kitchen. Would this affect my bargain with God? But no, I had to think that God wouldn't mind if Benjamín and I talked now and then. Just as friends.

"Benjamín," I called, glancing over my shoulder at the door, hoping no one would charge in.

He turned around and seemed surprised to see me there. He set the trays down and wiped his hands with a kitchen towel, then gave me his complete attention as if to say, *Okay, I'm here. Now, what are you going to say?*

"I'm sorry for what I said that time. I would like to be your friend, if that's—if, um, you still want to be mine." I said it all in a rush before I chickened out.

He looked at me as if trying to figure out if this was a joke.

"I've missed our conversations," I said.

"Yeah, me too," he said, slowly letting out his breath.

Had he been holding it, like me, all this time?

"But are you sure?"

I didn't blame him for not trusting me. Maybe I'd been too harsh at our last meeting. My breakup with him—or whatever it was—had been kind of weird. Maybe I'd shocked him and left him wondering whether he could ever trust me again. And even though the Almond Joys he'd given me continued to hold a treasured spot in the box with my diary, he didn't know that.

I nodded. "Yes, I—"

Just then one of his brothers came in. "Hey, there you are," he said. "Mom's looking for you." Then he noticed me. "Oh," he said. "I see you're busy." He wiggled his eyebrows at Benjamín and left.

"Brothers," he said, blushing.

I smiled.

"So, um, okay," he said. "Do you want to meet up sometime? Grab a 7UP?"

"Do you want to try Palm City Go-Karts?" I asked. "It finally opened."

"Sure," he said. "Just give me the Communion nod."

"I will," I said, smiling.

"There you are," Ana called, pushing the kitchen door wide open. "It's time to go." Then she noticed Benjamín. "Oh," she said. "Excusez-moi!" And she quickly turned around and left.

"Sisters," I said, and we both started laughing.

TWENTY-SEVEN

Who said miracles couldn't happen? First, Father Carrasco's secretary called Mamá the very next morning to say that Father Carrasco was going to resign as the Guadalupana adviser. Later that day I heard Mama talking to Tía Matilde over the phone.

"Father Stadler may not speak Spanish," she said about the new adviser, "but at least he'll be more respectful of our indigenous heritage." Then she added that she'd heard Father Carrasco had put in for a transfer to another parish. "I hope that is so," she said. I don't know what Tía said at the other end of the call, but Mamá responded: "I *had* to confront him, Matilde. As the president of the Guadalupanas, I felt it my duty to let him know his sermon had been disrespectful to his parishioners—calling our ancestors 'illiterate indios.' What arrogance!"

I wanted to hug Mamá right then and there. I was proud of how she'd taken a stand with the pastor. But I also wondered why she had. Was it her way of getting back at him for not writing the letter of recommendation for Chuy? Did she feel this was one time when she had some power to make changes? Maybe this was her way of dealing with the anger and sadness she must be feeling about Chuy being drafted.

And then the second miracle happened: snow in San Diego! We charged outside, laughing and shouting, "It's snow! It's really snowing!" We tried catching a few flakes, sticking our tongues out like frogs snagging an insect. I'd never in my life seen snow fall. And in our giddiness, my sisters and I twirling around in the middle of the street, I was sure this was a sign from God. Chuy was set to go to boot camp in less than three weeks, but miracles could and would happen.

Maybe the surprise snow flurries in our neighborhood inspired my parents, but for whatever reason (another miracle?), this year they splurged on a real Christmas tree instead of putting up our usual spindly aluminum one. On the front lawn we had a life-size plastic nativity scene of Mary, Joseph, and Baby Jesus while Christmas lights outlined the house. We were going all out with the decorations, Carolina explained to me, because Chuy would be leaving for boot camp and he'd invited his girlfriend, Donna, over for Christmas Eve.

Monica and Luz loved wrapping the prizes for the lotería winners: a new pair of socks, a round bar of Maja soap, a decorative dish towel, a hand mirror.

"Who'd you get this Christmas?" I heard Ana whisper to Carolina as they decorated the tree with ornaments.

"I heard you!" I called out to Ana. "It's called *secret* Santa for a reason."

"You're nothing but a metiche with big ears," she said, laughing.

Every year, we all secretly hoped Octavio picked our name. Mr. Lover Boy was as generous with his gifts to us as he was with sharing himself with multiple girlfriends. He always went beyond the ten-dollar limit. "At that rate, you'll never have enough money in your life, Octavio," Mamá warned him every Christmas. "Don't be so espléndido."

And every Christmas he was. One year it was a child-size kitchen set with refrigerator, stove, and oven. Another year—*my lucky Christmas year!*—he bought me a Barbie with three wigs and a gold lamé evening gown.

But now that I was preparing to be a nun, it'd be best if Octavio *hadn't* picked my name. It was never too soon to prepare for a future life of self-denial. It was time to stop hoping to be the recipient of espléndido gifts.

I examined our Douglas fir Christmas tree with its golden angel at the top and the blue, red, green, silver, and gold ornaments dangling from the spiky needles. As I inhaled the fresh piney smell, I imagined myself hiking through the Alps, singing along with the von Trapp family. And even if Carolina was right and the real-life von Trapps might not have escaped by walking over the Alps—"It's just a Hollywood movie, Yoli"—they *had* escaped a war they didn't believe in. That part had to be true, didn't it? And once again, all the gaiety—the positivity I'd been trying to hold on to—dipped and dissolved as quickly as the San Diego snowflakes.

∙ ∙ ∙

Christmas Eve at the Sahagún home: tamales, atole, eggnog, lotería, and Chuy with his love. Who could ask for more? This wasn't my first time meeting Donna, but seeing her in her Christmas holiday attire—well, she looked just like an angel. Pobrecita, it must've been overwhelming to have an army of people checking her out. She wore a white wool sweater with a red-white-and-green Scottish-style plaid skirt. A red velvet hairband crowned her long blond tresses. What was not to love? I soon had Ritchie Valens's "Donna" crooning in my head. I could only imagine what Chuy must've felt having this angel as his girlfriend. Tomorrow was Christmas Day, and Chuy was going to propose to her. Observing them, the way she looked dreamily into his eyes even as all eyes looked at *her*, I was sure she would say yes.

We made a huge fuss over her—well, at least *I* did. Even amid the annoyed looks of Ana and Carolina, I attended to My Lady with great enthusiasm. "Coke, 7UP?" I asked Donna. "Perhaps a glass of our delightful wine?"

Chuy looked at me, amused.

After dinner, we cleared and folded the tables and sat wherever we found space in the living room for a few rounds of lotería. Chuy and Donna sat on the orange love seat with their Mexican-style bingo cards on their laps and a handful of pinto beans as markers. I noticed he hadn't stopped smiling.

"¡Lotería!" Chuy called out, and when the pinto beans spilled onto the vinyl floor, they both laughed, those cutie-pie sweethearts. She looked into his blue eyes, he into hers. Surely, she would stand by him no matter what.

"It's almost midnight!" Luz proclaimed. The lotería game was over, and she'd been so patient. "Can we open the presents now?"

And we were off!

Shirts, pullover sweaters, flannel pajamas, socks, pantyhose, colored hairbands, Simon and Garfunkel's *Live from New York City, 1967* album, Wham-O Superball, and a box of decorative Maja soaps—la Noche Buena was a flurry of festive wrapping paper ripped and crumpled into balls, gasps, and happy shouts of *Oh, thank you*. I had picked Luz's name and gotten her the Pebbles and Bamm-Bamm paper dolls she'd been begging for. Lucky Monica won the jackpot: an Easy-Bake Oven from Octavio.

For Tía Matilde, we had all pooled our money and bought her a bedside lamp with a gold shade and a golden floral bedspread with matching cushions. Her bedroom would be one you'd find in the grand estates of England and Austria.

During the happy havoc of gift opening, I snuck glances at Chuy and Donna. He leaned over and whispered something to her. She nodded and smiled, leaned his way to say something back.

"To Yoli from Tía Matilde," Carolina called out, reading the gift tag.

I quickly unwrapped the package and found a floral, hardbound book of psalms. In loopy, elegant handwriting, Tía Matilde had inscribed it: *Querida Yolanda, may these psalms comfort, guide, and strengthen your resolve as you go forward in life. Con todo mi cariño, Tía Matilde.* I hugged my dear aunt. A most perfect gift, one that I would take with me to the canyon for peaceful reading, one that I would slip under my pillow after a silent night of praying.

• • •

Past midnight, when all of us were tucked safely in bed and not a creature was stirring, I jotted down one more thought in my diary: *Though really, Dear Diary, the only Christmas gift I ever truly wanted on this Holy Night was for General Westmoreland and President Johnson to declare—"Happy Christmas to all, and to all a good night!"—that the war was finally over.*

TWENTY-EIGHT

"So you'll have a sister-in-law, eh?" Lydia said.

"Yup," I said, trying to contain my excitement. (She'd said yes, yes, yes!)

We were walking over to Brown's Market for milk. My parents had gone shopping to Mercado Hidalgo in Tijuana that morning and bought a supply of our favorite item: seven yellow-and-red-striped hexagonal boxes of tablet chocolate. We'd promised Monica and Luz we'd teach them how to play Monopoly and include them in our chocolatito New Year's Eve party tomorrow.

Lydia and I picked four cartons of milk, paid the cashier at the front of the store, and walked out. It was a clear, nice day, so we took our time getting back to my house.

"So far I have four things on my resolution list," Lydia said. "What about you?"

"Just four?" I asked. "Heck, Lydia, I should think you'd have a billion."

"Oh, so funny," Lydia said. "You must have a trillion."

I gave her a look. "Seven," I said.

"What are they?" she asked.

"I'd rather not say," I said. "My resolutions are *my* resolutions. Is this a contest we're having?"

"Well, excuse me, Your Highness," she said. "I was just curious. You've been acting a little weird lately, all mysterious and serious." She paused, maybe hoping I'd fill in the blanks.

I didn't.

"May I suggest you put on your list *Be nice to Lydia like I used to be in the good old days.*"

"The *good old days*?" I started laughing. Sometimes Lydia could be funny.

I didn't want Lydia to know that Benjamín was back in my life. She'd been pleased with my announcement that I'd gotten him out of my system. It'd be hard enough telling her that I wasn't going to join her at the Our Lady of Angels convent in Pennsylvania. *A nun in Vietnam? Are you kidding me?* I could already hear her saying this, so why bring Benjamín into it?

"Are you going to tell me?" she asked. "Or are you going to continue to be all misteriosa?"

"Okay, okay, fine," I said. "I'll add your suggestion as an *eighth* resolution to my list. Happy already? But no, I'm not going to tell you what my resolutions are. I like to keep them a secret."

• • •

New Year's Resolutions for 1968:

Number 1: Say the rosary every night before going to sleep.

Number 2: Be aware of the news in the world.

Number 3: Be kind to my sisters—that includes no teasing or making fun of Drowsy Doll and Miss Pointy Boobs Barbie.

Number 4: During Lent, give up something more austere than bubble gum. Hot chocolate? Pan dulce? Almond Joys?

Number 5: Do better in math—at least a B.

Number 6: Be more helpful around the house and yard.

Number 7: Read one novel a week.

Number 8: Be nice to Lydia like I used to be in the good old days.

Had I been pushing Lydia away? And was it because of my friendship with Benjamín, or was the Chuy situation keeping me all misteriosa? Why hadn't I told Lydia what I was trying to do for Chuy? Was I afraid she'd laugh and think I was stupid for making a pact with God?

• • •

It was a warm, sunny last day of December, and Octavio, Tony, El Chango, and Chuy were sitting out on the patio. Getting a head start on New Year's resolution number 6, I volunteered to hang the laundry, mainly so I could overhear their conversation from my spot at the clothesline.

"A lottery system," I heard Octavio said. "There's talk of that, to make things fairer, you know."

"How is it fairer than what we have now?" Tony asked.

"Because everyone would be treated equally," said Chuy. "Whether rich or poor, a high school dropout, or a student at a fancy college."

"I still don't get it."

"Right now, if you're a full-time college student, you get a deferral. With the lottery system, all that goes away."

"I like it," said El Chango. "Rich and poor hunkered down next to each other in the foxholes."

• • •

Later that night, Luz, Monica, Lydia, and I set up the Monopoly board on the kitchen table, getting ready for our New Year's Eve game night, while Mamá was making us our chocolatito. She was standing at the stove, and I listened to the swishing of the wooden molinillo as she briskly rubbed the wooden handle in the clay pot, a whisking motion that produced foamy hot chocolate.

Tía Matilde, Carolina, Ana, Tony, and Papá were in the living room watching TV. Octavio was on what he called "a hot date," Chuy was hanging out with Donna and his friends at El Chango's house, and Armando was somewhere in the city of Madrid probably celebrating the New Year with other university students. Papá laughed at something they were watching on TV, and I was not only happy to see him laughing—something none of us were doing too much of lately—but glad that he had tomorrow off when Chuy left for boot camp.

I let Lydia be the banker, provided I got the silver roadster for my marker. I noticed that we each guarded our stacks of gold, beige, blue, green, yellow, pink, and white bills as if they were real. She and I explained the game to Luz and Monica as we played. We kept the explanation simple: "Whenever you land on a property," I told them, "buy it." I helped Luz manage her money, and Lydia helped Monica with hers. We were pretty much two teams.

A good hour passed when I struck it lucky. Park Place and Boardwalk were in my possession, plus the four railroad companies and a Get Out of Jail Free card. And once I purchased my first hotel, Lydia announced, "It's over. She won."

What did that mean? my little sisters wanted to know. Why was the game over?

"Yoli's the big land baron," Lydia explained to Luz and Monica.

I tried not to gloat about my winnings (lots of gold bills in my stack!).

When Chuy and El Chango walked in a few minutes later, I was the first to look up.

Huh?

"Well, what do you think?" they asked.

Both sides of their heads were completely shaved, leaving a long middle strip of hair from forehead to back of neck. Mohawk hairdos!

And then Mamá came out of the kitchen.

"Ay, por Dios, muchachos, what have you done?" she said.

"They're going to chop it all off tomorrow anyway," Chuy explained as he put his arm around Mamá. "Thought we'd have us some fun before things got too serious."

Soon Carolina and Ana rushed out of the bedroom, wondering what all the ruckus was about. There was laughter and picture taking—El Chango and Chuy posing for the camera—and doing all the things one did to make the joke extra funny and light. For this moment, gathered around them in the living room, we might forget what had led to the haircuts in the first place.

• • •

December 31, 1967. Chuy leaves for Fort Ord tomorrow, I wrote late that night. *What an awful way to start the New Year. If only I was a land baron! I'd sell my big, fancy hotel on Park Place to the highest bidder, add that money to my stack of five-hundred-dollar bills, and give it to Chuy and send him to Mexico on the next Tres Estrellas de Oro bus. I trust that 1968 will bring us all good luck.*

Four months of boot camp. It was just training, not the war, I reminded myself. Not yet.

• • •

The next day, Carolina warned us to put on a positive face. "No lloriqueos," she said, looking at me. "We're a strong, stoic family, Yoli. No wearing your heart on your sleeve, okay?"

Stoic? Heart on my sleeve?

Okay, fine, I got it: no crybabies.

"Hey, Yoli bo-boli," Chuy said when it was my turn for a good-bye hug. "Nothing but straight A's on your report card, okay, Miss Junior High Girl?"

I tried on a smile. I wanted to whisper in his ear that this whole boot camp training would be for nothing, that I had made a pact with God.

Then El Chango, with his twin Mohawk haircut, gave Chuy a strong, brotherly hug.

In a flash Chuy was in the car with Donna and Mamá and Papá, on his way to the airport. Fort Ord was in Northern California, not so far away, when you thought about it. Not as far away as Vietnam, for instance. Not as dangerous.

The car pulled out, and I watched as El Chango limped home. Without Chuy at his side, he looked incomplete and lost.

Didn't we all?

TWENTY-NINE

Benjamín and I met at the newly opened Palm City Go-Karts the following Sunday. Mamá had allowed me an hour instead of the usual thirty minutes because I'd done well on the California Achievement Test. The go-kart course was outdoors, and already I could see, as I biked up to Benjamín, a long line of squirmy kids waiting their turn to get on the go-karts. Adjacent to the course, a building housed a noisy, beeping arcade.

"Happy New Year!" he said.

"And to you!" I hadn't seen him since the Guadalupana party, not even at Mass. I figured he was out of town with his family.

As if he could read my mind, he said, "We went up to San Bruno and stayed with relatives during Christmas vacation."

"San Bruno?"

"It's in the Bay Area," he said. "My mom's sister. This tía is really religious and always begs my mom to come up and spend Christmas with her family. She does the whole posada thing. We walk around their neighborhood singing all the religious Christmas songs in English and Spanish. It's kind of fun, to be honest."

I nodded. Then: "I'm going to be a nun when I grow up." Better to get it out in the open right away.

"Oh, yeah?" He looked at me strangely.

"Yeah," I said. "You seem surprised."

"I *am* surprised," he said. "No offense, but you don't seem the type."

"What do you mean?" I asked.

I noticed one kid in line was shoving an older one, who looked like he could be his brother.

"Can't explain it," he said. "I've just been around a lot of nuns, and you don't seem the type. Don't get me wrong," he added. "I like nuns and have a lot of respect for them, especially if they're cool like my teacher Sister Marie. But most of them are serious—too serious—about life and prayers and keeping within strict Catholic rules. Not like you."

I looked at Benjamín. "But I *am* going to be a nun," I said. "And I'm going to be a darn good one."

"Oh, okay," he said, raising his hands in surrender. "Sorry."

"No, that's fine," I said. "I appreciate your honesty."

We were quiet after that. I noticed that the older brother got tired of the younger's pushing. He suddenly pushed him back, and the little kid fell on his butt. He didn't cry, though.

"So maybe I should become a priest," he said. Those eyes, that smile. "This way maybe we can work at the same parish."

"I'm going to be a missionary nun in Vietnam," I blurted.

"Huh?"

Stupid, stupid me. What the heck was I doing divulging all this stuff to him? Even Lydia didn't know my secret plans.

"Nobody knows this," I said as an afterthought.

At least I hadn't revealed my pact with God. I wasn't *that* stupid.

"Your secret's safe with me, Yoli," he said.

And I trusted him. This was the same guy who had cleaned my dirty shoe, who said I was the prettiest girl at the party. I believed he wouldn't tell anyone.

I asked him if any of his brothers were going to be sent to Vietnam.

"No, my oldest isn't yet eighteen." He looked at me. "I heard your brother is in boot camp right now."

I nodded, realizing I didn't want to talk about it—the whole thing with war and soldiers. And maybe he understood that, too, because he suddenly asked if I wanted to ride the go-karts. "I bought us tickets," he said.

So we did. We drove this way and that on the curvy course, and at one point I bumped into a few car tires that bordered the course and it slowed my cart, and Benjamín, who'd been driving respectfully behind me, saw his chance and zoomed past, laughing and waving to me. And then I got going again, trying to catch up with Benjamín. This was as exhilarating as when Chuy let me test-drive his homemade go-kart when I was young.

But soon—too soon—the red light on a pole in the center of the course began blinking, our cue to slow down and drive back to the home station. The attendant waved us in as well.

"I have to go home," I said as soon as we got out of the carts and headed to the exit. "It's getting late."

"Next time we meet," he said, "can we meet here?"

"Yes," I said. "That sounds great."

I hopped on my bike and waved to him. He smiled his Frankie Avalon smile.

But all the way up Hollister Street, a nagging thought poked at me. A pact with God? Was this the right way to get what I wanted?

• • •

"What'd you do yesterday?" Lydia asked as soon as I caught up with her on the tracks, headed for school. We had raincoats on.

"Do you think it's going to rain hard today?" I asked her as I contemplated the mean-looking clouds.

She looked at me. "First off, I asked you a question," she said. "And you answered by talking about the weather. Makes me think you're avoiding my question. What gives with you, Yoli?"

"I don't have to give you an accounting of what I did yesterday or any other day," I said. "What are you, a private detective or something? Did I commit a crime? What gives with *you*?"

"Man," she said. "You've been one royal grump, and I'm getting sick and tired of it. I'll tell you what. When you decide to keep your resolution and *be nice to Lydia like in the good old days*, give me a call. Until then, let's just stay out of each other's way. Oh, and by the way," she added. "That flimsy raincoat you're wearing? It will do you no good for the Pennsylvania winters." And with that, she took off in a sprint with heavy textbooks and all.

I felt like shouting out after her: *I'm not going to the convent in Pennsylvania, tonta! I'm going to be serving Our Lord in the tropical jungles of Vietnam, just for your information—and a flimsy raincoat is exactly what I'll need!* I stopped and watched as she quickly and skillfully stepped over the wooden railroad ties.

I guessed I really had become something of a grouch. Instead of sharing things with my best friend—my pact with God, my friendship with Benjamín—I was shutting her out.

• • •

After school I walked home alone, and when I got to the house, I let the screen door slam behind me.

"Hey, Yoli, check this out." Tony was sitting cross-legged on the floor, a stack of albums and singles in front of him. He looked like the owner of a record store, taking inventory of his music treasures.

"Tony, I'm kind of not in the mood to listen to music right now," I said. "Not even the Monkees."

"Uyy," he said. "That's not a good sign."

Maybe I needed to have a snack—a warm corn tortilla with melted butter and a sprinkling of salt? An apple? One of Ana's homemade oatmeal cookies? Something to stop me from thinking of my conversation with Lydia and our crumbling friendship.

"Just listen to this one." He quickly placed the needle on an album. Simon and Garfunkel's "Scarborough Fair" began playing.

As I listened, Tony kept looking at me as if he expected me to react in some way. When the song was over, he asked, "Well, what did you think? Did you get it?"

I shook my head no.

"It's about war, Yoli," he said. "It took me a couple of days to figure out the hidden lyrics, but here." He handed me a paper where he'd written them down.

I sat down and read, coming to the last line about generals ordering their soldiers to kill and to fight for a cause they'd long forgotten. It was a whisper of a prayer, a sad chant.

I looked up at Tony. My eyes were glassy with tears. "Can I listen to it again?"

THIRTY

A whole month had gone by and nothing from Lydia. Fine. If she wanted to be mad at me, then I could be mad at her, too. We avoided each other in English class and PE. After all, two could play the game.

On Saturday, four days before Valentine's Day, Carolina drove Luz, Monica, and me to Kresge's. Now that Luz was in first grade, I was as excited as she was for her very first school Valentine's Day party.

"I want a lot of Pebbles and Bamm-Bamm cards," she said, as if she were already an authority on Valentine's Day cards.

Third-grader Monica went straight to the packet of *Jetsons* cards.

I, on the other hand, took my time, wanting to relay just the right message—nothing too cutesy, nothing too mushy and juvenile. I'd done this every February for the past six years—deciding which set of Valentines would strike the right chord.

"Yoli, could you please just hurry up and pick something?" Luz piped in.

It was, after all, her first Valentine's Day party, whereas I was a veteran of cupid's arrow and the swirls of red hearts, of pretty mermaids plunging into the depths of the ocean claiming, *Valentine, deep down I need you.*

"Okay, okay," I said as I picked a thirty-six pack of *Peanuts* Valentines.

"Oh, you too, Yoli?" Carolina asked as she handed the money to the cashier.

I was pleased with my choice. Snoopy, Charlie Brown, and Peppermint Patty were my favorite characters. Seated next to Carolina in the car as we headed home, I glanced at her, grateful that she'd volunteered to drive us to the store. If I had any left over, I'd be sure to give our resident psychologist one of my Lucy ones.

I poked through my box of cards, figuring out who would be on my list of recipients. Classmates in my homeroom period? A possibility. Sneak a card into the notebook binder of that cute guy Renato in geography? Why not? How about some of the girls in PE—slip a Valentine into their gym lockers, including the locker of one particular person who was presently *not* my best friend? Knowing Lydia, she'd probably just ignore it and pretend she'd never received it.

And then it hit me, why Carolina had asked me that question.

Classroom Valentine's Day cards? What was I thinking? I'd be the laughingstock of Southwest Junior High. Yoli is passing out *Valentine's Day* cards to all her classmates—like she's in *elementary school.* Hee-hee. Yolanda Sahagún, Doofus of the Century.

The rest of the way home, I miserably looked out the side window as we passed the pepper-tree-lined streets in Chula Vista. If only I could be transported to one of these trees. I'd become a red-tailed hawk, hunt rats and other nasty rodents, and fly my way to the rest of my life, never to be found again. From my perch on the highest branch, I'd look down at the little houses, like the green Monopoly ones, and wonder what it was like to be squished in one of those boxes, to go in and out of them—as it seemed humans did all the time—with schedules and duties and thoughts unknown to me as a bird soaring in the sky, just looking for my next meal and a place to safely nest.

We turned off Hollister onto Conifer Street.

Try as I might in my daydreams—imagining a different kind of life for myself—I was a person and not a bird. I closed the packet, figuring I'd give the cards away to some little neighbor kid or keep them for Monica or Luz to use next year. Sometimes growing up was no fun.

• • •

The only nod at school to Saint Valentine came from the hamburger-smelling cafeteria offering red velvet cupcakes with a candy heart nestled in the vanilla frosting. Fifteen cents apiece—oh, whoop-dee-do!

My soggy sandwich of bologna, mayonnaise, lettuce, and tomato, along with a slightly bruised red apple and a mini carton of milk would suffice.

In PE, Lydia and I kept our distance. Suzy and I jogged around the track, and I could tell she was trying to keep me entertained with stories of Reilly's doggy exploits, but nobody could entertain me with her goofy comments like Lydia. Still, I was grateful to Suzy for trying. I glanced at Lydia, a lap ahead of us, who seemed (I hoped) equally bored listening to Mean Mary Ann.

As I half listened to Suzy, I wondered what advice Chuy would give me about Lydia, how to mend our friendship. Would he tell me to be honest with her? Even though Chuy didn't know about my pact with God, he'd probably say I should level with her. Chuy was like that. He'd tell the truth.

• • •

Once I was home, Luz called as she rushed to meet me at the front door, "Guess what came in the mail!"

She held out a large manila envelope addressed to the Sahagún family. I studied the return address:

J. Sahagún US 56715579 F-2-4 (C.S.T.)
Fort Ord. CAL 93941 Class 471

"Well, hurry up and open it, for Pete's sake," I demanded, about to burst.

Luz opened the envelope and pulled out five smaller envelopes hand-printed with our names, one for each sister. "Here's yours," she said.

Miss Yolanda Sahagún. I recognized Chuy's clean, meticulous handwriting. I ripped open the envelope. The Valentine's Day card showed Snoopy with a pointer stick standing next to a blackboard with dates on it. *You'll probably go down in history...*, the front said. Turning it over, I read, "...as one of the world's nicest Valentines. *Love you, hermanita—Chuy.*"

Dropping my textbooks on the sofa, I ran outside and across the street to my tree with Chuy's Valentine in hand. And once I was comfortably settled on the platform, I examined the card carefully. Grinning Snoopy in his red bow tie, looking every bit a distinguished professor, was pointing his stick at dates on the chalkboard: 1492, 1776, and 1812.

I was certain that the war would be over soon and that next year Chuy would be handing us our Valentine's Day cards in person.

• • •

Two weeks later, Socorrito rang us up and shouted into the phone: "Turn on your TV to Walter Cronkite. *Now!*" Then she hung up.

I quickly turned on the TV while calling out to everyone to come and hear.

Our favorite TV anchor was reading a statement on air to the American people because he'd just returned from covering the war in Vietnam. When he finished talking, Carolina looked at Octavio. "Wow, I hope they take his advice."

Octavio nodded.

"I didn't understand," Monica said. "What did he mean?"

"Mr. Cronkite thinks that it's time that South Vietnam and the United States negotiate with North Vietnam."

"But what does *negotiate* mean?" asked Luz.

Carolina paused, probably thinking of a way to put it into simple terms. Then she said, "It means that everybody who is fighting each other should talk and agree to stop fighting. To end the war."

"If they do negotiate, it means the war will be over soon, right?" I asked. "And Chuy won't need Fort Ord training anymore."

Carolina and Octavio nodded.

Soon everyone jumped in, excited.

"And we'll have a party to celebrate the end of the war!"

"Can we call him up and tell him about Walter Cronkite's report?"

"How soon will Chuy be back home?"

"Then he can marry Donna right away!"

I was too excited to stay still. But since I wasn't talking to Lydia, I made for the front door and ran over to Don Epifranio's house.

I knocked on his wooden screen door. "Don Epifranio," I called out in a loud, happy, sing-songy voice.

The hills and the canyon and my pepper tree are alive with the sound of music!

"Don Epi—"

"Ya voy," he called out in his croaky, beautiful viejito voice. "Ya voy!"

And when he reached the door, he started laughing and nodding. "Yes, niña," he said as he came out into the twilight-filled porch. "I know why you're here. Socorrito called me, too."

He pointed with his cane for me to sit on the other porch chair. "Let's just hope that Washington heard the report, too—and that they get to the negotiation table ahora mismo."

Darkness settled in softly. February evenings—this February evening!—could be as hopeful and full of light as in April.

Don Epifranio pointed to the sky in the east. "La luna," he announced, as if he were the caller in a Mexican lotería game. "El farol de los enamorados. *And*, I might add," he said, smiling and looking at me, "the lantern of the hopeful dreamers."

The gibbous moon held the promise of a splendid full moon tomorrow, for the kind of illumination our nation desperately needed.

THIRTY-ONE

Lydia continued to ignore me. As soon as she put on her gym suit, socks, and sneakers, she'd quickly join a group of other girls, laughing and talking with them as we all headed out to the track. The way she deliberately avoided me made me wonder if she'd given me up for Lent.

Same thing in our English class. She'd slip into the chair of her desk at the other end of the room and never once glanced my way, not even when Mrs. Benson shushed and scolded Dorky Alan, who sat next to me. I seriously doubted that Lydia's rapt attention on the difference between adjectives and adverbs was for real.

Mrs. B. tried making the lessons interesting, with team games meant to spark a dose of competition among us. "Call out as many adverbs as you can in fifteen seconds," she instructed my team. "Yoli," she said. "Your turn. On your mark, get set, go!"

And I was on: *Kindly. Regretfully. Sorrowfully. Apologetically. Sadly. Confusedly. Hopefully.* I glanced at Lydia.

"Good, good!" Mrs. B. called out, looking at her stopwatch. "Eight seconds left, keep it up!"

Desperately. Truthfully. Remorsefully. Repentantly. Belatedly. Contritely. Devoutly.

My teammates looked at each other.

"Three more seconds!"

Prayerfully. Penitently. Peacefully.

Was that a smile on Lydia's face?

"Time!" Mrs. B. said as the bell rang for class to end. "Yoli's team wins."

As we piled out, I glanced at Lydia. She was actually grinning at me.

• • •

"Vietnam?" Lydia demanded as we walked home on the tracks. "Why the heck didn't you just tell me?" As usual, Lydia avoided stepping on the railroad ties, as if they were the cracks that would break her mother's back.

"I didn't want to hurt your feelings," I said. "Or disappoint you. Remember, we've been planning this since we were eight years old."

"Of course I remember," she said, kicking a fat pebble. "And yeah, I think you're being ridiculous, and yeah, I *am* hurt about this. It seems like a dumb plan, Yoli. Really."

"I'm sorry, Lydia."

"Instead of being sorry," she said, "just forget about Vietnam. Our Lady of Angels convent awaits us."

I didn't say anything.

"Tell me again: Why Vietnam?" She stared at me as if the body snatchers had finally taken hold of me.

I hadn't fully thought this part out, how to explain to her the Vietnam missionary work without giving away my promise to God. I was hopeful the war would be over any day now, and I didn't want to jinx the pact by revealing it to anyone, not even to my best friend.

"I want a real challenge," I said. "To help rebuild what we're destroying. And since Vietnam will be repairing itself for years after this war ends, I thought that might be the place—"

Lydia shook her head. "You could've at least consulted with me before making these grand separate plans of yours. It seems so random and sudden. Weird."

I glanced behind me, thinking I'd heard a train. But no, there was nothing. Just Lydia and me on the tracks headed home, someday down different paths.

"Our Lady of Angels seems like such a neat convent, and we'd be doing purposeful work in our own country, Yoli. But..." She didn't finish her sentence. She looked at me as if trying to figure me out.

"But what?" I asked.

"There's something more you're hiding from me, isn't there?"

She knew me too well. And if we were going to continue being best friends, I had to fess up.

"Benjamín and I are talking again," I said.

"Yeah, I figured as much," she said. "What's the big deal? So, he's back to being your friend. Okay, fine."

"I didn't want you to think I was being wishy-washy about being a nun. That I wasn't truly committed to my future vocation."

"You know, Yoli," she said, "I don't doubt your commitment. We're going to make the greatest nuns ever! Maybe even reach saint status—we're going to be that good."

"You think?" I smiled at her. Lydia, always the optimist.

"I know!" she said. "But in the meantime, we need to get these tontos out of our system."

I started laughing.

"Really," she said. "I mean it. And then we're going to be far-out nuns!"

• • •

The month of March was almost over, and I hadn't had a chance to catch my breath. The tons of homework due before Easter break filled my brain. As I came to my front gate, I heard Socorrito mumbling something and shaking her head as she stood under her large jacaranda tree.

"Hello, Socorrito," I called out to her.

"Un desmadre is what we have," she said. "Violence and death and so many injured."

I'd never seen her look so shook up. "In Vietnam?" I asked.

"No, Yoli," she said. "I'm talking about *here*, in this United States of America. Memphis, Tennessee. A peaceful civil rights march led by the Reverend Martin Luther King Jr. The cops beating up on the Blacks. It's war abroad *and* here."

"Is Dr. King okay?" I asked. "Did he get hurt in the riot?"

"No, he's fine, gracias a Dios."

I was still hoping Dr. King would get us out of this mess. I hadn't forgotten his TV interview last summer. He would persist, and soon—oh, yes, soon!—the politicians would come to their senses and finally end the war.

Socorrito was looking up at the bare branches of her tree. It was the end of March, but soon lavender shoots would appear, preparing for the full spray of bell-shaped blossoms in June. "Un desmadre," she mumbled to herself, shaking her head. "That's all I'm going to say about it."

• • •

Chuy returned from Fort Ord on the last day of March. Hugs, laughter, little-sister twirls around him. *What was the worst part of it? The best part? Did he meet Gomer Pyle? Was his sergeant loud and grumpy like Sergeant Carter? You look so thin! Don't they feed you enough?*

And he did look thin. And tired. And I wondered what he was thinking, what he had experienced in boot camp. Did whatever happened in boot camp make him feel more confident the war would soon end or not? Had he changed his mind and decided that heading to Mexico was the best choice?

My brothers had tons of questions for Chuy about his infantry training, but Mamá shushed everyone. "Let's watch President Johnson's speech, then eat," she said. "Questions later."

We all gathered around the TV console to listen, including Papá and Tía Matilde, whom we had invited over to welcome Chuy back.

...first step to de-escalate the conflict...reducing—substantially reducing—the present level of hostilities...bring about a reduction in level of violence that now exists.

"What does—" Monica was quickly shushed and told *later* by Carolina.

I knew it meant our president wanted to slow down the war and get out. I knew it meant that he wanted to negotiate with North Vietnam, and I knew it meant that Chuy would probably *not* be sent to Vietnam in three weeks after all. Oh, yes, hooray!

I looked at the others, and I could see there were signs of relief all around: Mamá clasping her hands as if in grateful prayer; Papá nodding slowly, looking relieved; and Tía Matilde clicking her knitting needles together at a happy pace. Tony and Octavio gave Chuy a brotherly pat on the back. Caro and Ana were grinning.

But there was more.

...we and the other allied nations are contributing six hundred thousand fighting men to assist seven hundred thousand South Vietnamese troops in defending their little country.

Wait, what? Six hundred thousand more troops? Didn't he just say that he was de-escalating?

Chuy did not take his gaze off the TV. He seemed to deliberately avoid our looks.

We stared at the TV, at the bespectacled leader. Our president looked old and tired—probably as tired as everyone else in this country who wanted this war to be over.

When the president finished talking, we turned off the TV and arranged ourselves in the living room with either TV trays in place or dinner plates on our lap.

"What was boot camp like, mi'jo?" Papá asked.

"Are you sure you all want to hear?" he asked. "There were some rough times, I won't lie."

"Yes, yes," we said in chorus.

"But share whatever you want to share," Mamá said.

"The best times were the marching cadences we had to sing," he said, smiling. "Like 'Hip Hop Lollipop.'"

Luz and Monica immediately begged to be taught how to march to "Hip Hop Lollipop." And before the evening was over, he had them stomping in step through the living room, out the back door, onto the patio, into the yard, and then back around to the front yard and in through the door with precise, surefooted steps.

Hip hop lollipop—Let me hear your left drop—That sounded mighty fine—Let me hear it three more times.

The next week Luz and Monica gathered a Pied Piper–like following of eager little soldiers marching in cadence to "Hip Hop Lollipop"—even el travieso Georgie the Pest took time out from his usual mischief to march with the rest. Next to him, faithful Lobo shook his tail in rhythm to the marching. They all chanted in quick time as they headed purposefully down Conifer Street. *Hip hop clippity clap—Let me hear your fingers snap—That sounded mighty fine—Let me hear it three more times—Hip hop bellyache—Let me see your booty shake—That looked mighty fine—Let me see it three more times.*

THIRTY-TWO

It was Thursday and I was still pondering President Johnson's speech and what it would mean for Chuy and my pact with God. I was sitting in the living room that late afternoon staring at the glass coffee table with its crack in the middle. I was confused.

Someone was banging on the door, shouting, "Did you hear? Did you hear?"

Monica darted to the door. Socorrito was shaking, tears clouding her eyes. She grasped on to Monica to steady herself.

"He's dead!" she shouted. "Asesinado."

"Who?" "What are you talking about?" "Calm down." "Here, sit down." Speaking all at once, we ushered her into the house.

"Doctor...," she wailed, barely able to get the name out, her voice thick with emotion. "Dr. King, Martin Luther King Jr.!"

Mamá made the Sign of the Cross.

"On a balcony," Socorrito was saying between sobbing hiccups. "In Memphis. Pobrecito."

Mamá told me to bring Socorrito a glass of water. She was pale, looked ready to faint. I ran to the kitchen and my hand shook as I held the glass under the tap. This was it, then. This was how it would be. Did it mean—what was the phrase he'd used?—the *moral conscience* of our country was dead?

I felt sick to my stomach. I hurried back to the living room and placed the glass in Socorrito's hands, folding her fingers around it. The TV was on, and on the screen there was a photo of three men on a balcony pointing to their right.

I stole across the living room and out the back door, silently closing it behind me.

• • •

The mocking caw of a black crow. I started and glanced around. How had I gotten here? I didn't remember crossing the street to my canyon and climbing down the wooden-step perch. I held my diary in one hand and the brochure about Our Lady of Angels convent in the other.

A bloody war. Futile. Unjust. Dr. King's words were firmly planted in my mind.

The sour grass was sprouting as never before, the field carpeted with long, bright shoots of yellow flowers. Like a postcard from the Alps, a movie shot in the Austrian countryside.

Not a single patch of tired brown, not one remnant of winter's quiet sleep. Everything was alive and brilliant, and it disgusted me. I wanted mean, scratchy-thorn tumbleweed to whip into action. I wanted to scream and caw back at the crows.

I had thought Reverend King might be able to steer us out of the war. Now he was dead.

Making deals with God—who did I think I was? A new adverb pushed into my mind: *arrogantly*. To think I could make a pact with God and then all would be well in the world. *Yolanda Sahagún arrogantly made a pact with God.*

I studied the brochure in my hand. The pretty young woman on the cover looked toward the heavens, ready to receive the Lord, to become his bride. I had stopped wanting to become a nun, and God knew it, knew it all along. But I'd pushed ahead and *arrogantly* made a deal with him. What a hypocrite I was!

Methodically, I ripped the brochure in half, and then again and again until there was only a pile of small paper scraps, and just as quickly, I flung the torn pieces, watching them flitter through the air and land snowflake-like here and there in the picture-perfect canyon.

I opened my diary and positioned my pen, pausing a moment. I knew that what I was about to write would wipe away all the positive thinking Miss Toscano had tried to teach us. But I wasn't in sixth grade anymore, and there came a time—like now—when you had to face reality. *April 4, 1968. I know it now for sure*, I wrote. *This war is never going to end.*

• • •

On Palm Sunday, three days after Dr. King's assassination, I marched into church with my family, intent on begging with my whole heart and soul for some kind of miracle. This time, no pacts with God, no wheeling and dealing. Just honest-to-goodness praying.

When I went up to receive Communion, Benjamín gave me a slight nod. *Go-kart meeting at two o'clock today.* I nodded my *okay* back.

• • •

The thing about April was that it was moody. It could be brilliant and warm one day and gloomy and rainy the next. Kind of like me and how I was feeling as I bicycled over to the go-karts: gloomy, rainy, and moody.

Benjamín was already there, sitting on the wooden fence, swinging his legs. He waved to me, and I waved back as I rode up next to his bike. I was out of breath from the fast ride over and didn't say anything at first. Just gave him a kind of smile.

"You okay, Yoli?" he asked.

And that's all it took, that question and the sincere concern on his face. Stupid tears were trickling down my face.

I told him how sad I was about Dr. King's death. What I still *didn't* tell Benjamín was about my pact with God. I was too ashamed of myself.

"Sometimes I get so sad and angry that I just want to push off on my bike and ride and ride and do some daredevil things," I said.

He looked at me. "What do you mean?"

"Like," I said, scanning Hollister Street and beyond, "like ride down Suicide Hill as fast as I can."

"Yeah." He chuckled. "That'd be a daredevil thing to do."

"Have you ever done it, bicycled over Suicide Hill?" I asked him.

He shook his head. "No," he said. "My mom said if she ever heard that we had, she'd—" He stopped. "Your brothers do it, don't they?"

"Well, Chuy and his friend El Chango do," I said. "They're not supposed to, but they do it a lot."

"Pretty dangerous, isn't it?"

"Yeah," I said. "That's why they do it."

We were quiet for a long time. It seemed like words could never express what I was feeling, so why say anything?

"I can see you're sad, Yoli," Benjamín said. "Is there anything I can say to make you feel better?"

I smiled. I had to hand it to him: he sure did seem to understand my moods.

Then he asked me what our Easter tradition was, whether I still looked for hidden Easter eggs and all that. I could tell he was trying to cheer me up.

"Yes," I said. "All my sisters do. But we let Monica and Luz have a five-minute head start."

And him, what did he and his family do? "Same thing. We let our little brothers go first."

The go-kart line was growing.

"Are you still going to be a nun?" he asked.

I didn't answer right away. The go-karts zipped around the track as if they were in the Indianapolis 500.

I thought about President Johnson's speech—the part about

reducing the level of hostilities and the part about contributing six hundred thousand fighters. I kept trying to come up with a word for how I felt. *Trepidation?*

I looked at Benjamín. "Well," I said, "I...um...yeah, sure."

He looked at me. "That didn't sound convincing," he said, chuckling.

I looked at him. I wanted to tell him the truth. He'd be kind and understanding, I knew that. But I also knew this wouldn't be fair to Lydia, who'd been my best friend forever. She needed to know before him.

THIRTY-THREE

Lunar eclipse. Blood moon. Good Friday. It seemed a perfect combination—as if the moon and planet Earth were signaling something greater.

That evening, everyone left for Saint Charles except Chuy and me. I had a sore throat and Chuy had a cold. The house was unusually quiet because during Holy Week we had to limit our TV watching—especially on Good Friday. If Jesus could die on the cross for us, was our parents' argument, then we could certainly go one day without watching TV.

I was sitting in the living room curled up on the couch reading my book of psalms, while Chuy was in the kitchen boiling water and mint leaves—Mama's té de hierba buena was her antidote for everything. I watched as he poured the hot liquid into two cups. Then he added a teaspoonful of honey in each mug and stirred gently.

"Come and get it," he called out to me. I hurried into the kitchen.

"Thank you, Chuy," I said, sitting across from him at the kitchen table. Both of us were blowing on the hot tea.

I looked up at him. He only had a couple of weeks before leaving for Vietnam. "Where's Donna?" I asked. "It's going to be a romantic moon tonight. Why aren't you with her?"

She was spending a few days in Arizona with her father and stepmother, he explained. "She'll be back on Easter."

I nodded.

"A full moon tonight?" he asked.

"A blood moon, *and* an eclipse," I said.

He finished his tea before I did, but then just sat at the kitchen table, thinking. When he noticed that I had finished, he said, "Up for a little adventure this night of a blood moon?"

"You bet!" I said. The tea had soothed my throat.

I followed him out back to our bikes. As I reached for mine, he said, "Tell you what. Let's just take mine. This way I don't have to worry if you're keeping up."

As a little girl, I'd had plenty of practice hitching a ride on my brothers' bikes. I could expertly climb on the front wheel and then position myself on the handlebars or sit sidesaddle on the crossbar.

"Can you see okay?" I asked him.

"Yup."

"Where are we going?"

"Let's go for the grand view," he said.

And we headed to Suicide Hill.

Chuy and I walked the bike up the hill. It was a steep climb, and I was out of breath by the time we reached the top. I'd expected to see a traffic jam of cars parked along the shoulder, because this was the perfect spot for watching the phases of the eclipse. But no, we were the only ones here—as if we'd landed on a deserted planet. Eerie.

The spring evening sky was a clean, deep blue, and the moon had risen over the east county hills. Already you could see a small shadow taking a bite out of the yellow disk. We were silent for a long time, the night air growing colder. I shivered.

"We better get back before everyone returns from church," Chuy said.

"Can we ride down?" I asked.

He shook his head. "No, Yoli. It's too dangerous. We only came up here to see the view. That's all."

We both knew Mamá and Papá would murder us—that is, if we made it to the bottom alive.

"I'll hold on tight, I promise."

Chuy seemed to be thinking, considering. I waited.

"I want to feel the freedom," I said to him as the shadow extended its reach.

Because what was left? A war without an end and a brother soon to be pulled into it? A foolish pact with God? How childish of me! How naïve!

He looked at me, hesitating.

I pictured my family this very moment, kneeling in prayer in church, reciting the Stations of the Cross—Jesus Christ's progression to his crucifixion—while I was here with my beloved brother on an uncertain journey of our own.

Then he nodded.

I hopped on the crossbar, and Chuy directed me to place my hands on the inner part of the handlebars. He placed his on the brake levers.

Then he pushed off.

My god, what a ride! The cold air whipped my face, a blur of lights somewhere in another world, the menthol smell of eucalyptus trees nearby. I wanted to shout out with joy or fear or something, but I couldn't breathe—the sensation of being totally out of control gripped my whole body.

Death by hill? Death by accident? Death by war?

Promise me, God, that this will be the worst of it. This terror, this inability to catch my breath. Frightened way past screaming, I held on for dear life. Had I ever plunged to such depths? Had I ever wondered what heaven or hell would offer me?

I saw sky and moon, and then we were in a sudden, wide flip, a bicycle cartwheel, the world turned topsy-turvy. We nose-dived and crashed, the universe suddenly silent as my head hit the asphalt: the taste of dirt and blood, the grains of gravel in my mouth. My body sore and unmoving. Had I died? Had *we* died?

Yoli, Yoli.

I heard his voice. My favorite brother was calling out to me from somewhere far—from San Francisco with flowers in his hair? In

Vietnam, where soldiers clean and polish guns, sleep unaware of the clarion call? *Hip hop clippity clap—Let me hear your fingers snap!*

I opened my eyes. It was cold and I was shivering uncontrollably, a metallic taste in my mouth.

Chuy's face came into focus, hovering over me. "Yoli," he said. "Yoli, are you okay? Can you hear me?" What was wrong with his voice? It sounded thick, as if he was going to cry.

Don't cry, Chuy, I wanted to say. *Everything's gonna be okay. You gotta keep the faith, remember?* But my body hurt all over and I couldn't move.

I forced my eyes to focus.

Two guys were standing near us. They offered to walk the bike back as Chuy picked me up and carried me.

"I'm okay," I whispered to Chuy all the way up and over Suicide Hill. "Really, I'm okay, Chuy. I can walk on my own. I'm sure I can."

He was silent as he carried me with the care and gentleness of a parent with his newborn baby.

I heard the two guys talking to each other about our crash, something about how we just zoomed down as if we'd been flying, they'd never seen anyone ride that fast. Probably broke speeding records. Chuy didn't comment on their remarks. Once we got to Brown's Market, he told them he could take it from there. Just before they left, they said something to Chuy about how they believed in miracles now, that was one hell of a righteous ride. He waved and thanked them.

I was able to stand. I stood and wobbled for a moment, Chuy's hand on my arm steadying me.

"You sure you're okay?" he asked. "Do you feel dizzy or anything?"

I shook my head, not confident I could reassure him with words. He had blood smeared on his cheek.

"Lean against the bike and the wall, okay, Yoli? I'll be right back." As he walked into Brown's Market, I noticed he was limping. Was he hurt enough to get a medical deferment? Could this be the miracle I was praying for?

I glanced at the moon. Full eclipse. And we were alive, still here to tell the story. I leaned my head against the wall and closed my eyes. What was also left was a family who loved each other very much.

Cotton balls, rubbing alcohol, mercurio, Band-Aids, along with throat lozenges and decongestant pills. With the bike leaning against the store's wall, I sat on the seat as Chuy knelt and began first-aid preparations. There was one deep gash on my left elbow, a few smaller cuts on both hands, another near my mouth.

He ripped opened the plastic bag of cotton balls. "I'm so sorry to have done this, Yoli," he said. "It was a stupid thing I did. I should've known better. You could've gotten killed."

That thick voice of his. *Don't cry, Chuy,* I wanted to say.

"It was fun," I said, trying to cheer him up. "I felt the freedom, Chuy. I really did."

"No, Yoli," he said. "It was a royal pendejada on my part. I am so sorry, hermanita."

He doused the cotton balls with alcohol. "It's going to sting a bit," he warned as he patted the wet cotton on the wounds, wiping off the gravel and dirt. The blood.

And I started to cry. First just a little bit, and then I couldn't catch my breath, I was sobbing in gulps.

"Sorry," he said, quickly blowing on the cuts. "I know it hurts, Yoli. It'll stop in a couple of seconds. You're pretty banged up."

"That's not why I'm crying, Chuy," I said. "You know that's not why I'm crying."

He dabbed the mercurio on the cuts and then unwrapped the Band-Aids, applying one to each gash—gently, carefully—as if he were performing delicate surgery. He avoided my eyes.

"Promise me that you'll come back, Chuy," I said. "Promise me that."

"You know I can't promise you that, Yoli," he said.

He crumpled the Band-Aid wrappers and dropped them in the brown paper bag along with the bloodied cotton balls. He closed the cap on the alcohol bottle.

All the way back, he didn't say a word. I sat on the bike as he walked beside it, both of us holding on to the handlebars as he steered us home.

THIRTY-FOUR

The story we made up that night when they returned from Mass was that we'd decided to ride our bicycles over to Brown's Market to buy some throat lozenges and a decongestant. We didn't notice the tumbleweed as we turned onto Hollister—it was dark by then, we claimed.

"We crashed into an orchard of dead thorny brush, and fell off our bikes," I said. "It was really creepy." I was getting into my story. "Like the tumbleweed was lurking in the shadows, just waiting to attack us."

Chuy glanced at me. "Yeah, it was kind of weird," he said to Mamá.

She looked at me, then at Chuy, and then back to me. She wasn't buying it, I could tell. But she knew there was no way to get the real story once Chuy and I stood firmly next to each other.

"Thank God you didn't get killed," she said as she took off her black lace head covering and set her purse on the couch. She went into the kitchen to make us some more té de hierba buena.

The rest stood staring at my elbow, hands, and mouth, the red mercurio stains outlining the Band-Aids.

"Jeez, Yoli," Tony said. "It looks like you have ringworms or something."

"Dark on a full-moon night? Tumbleweed attacking you?" Carolina asked, shaking her head like Mamá. "No," Carolina whispered, looking at both Chuy and me. "It looks like you two have a bad case—no, an *amateurish* case—of non-truthitis."

• • •

Early the next morning, Chuy tapped me on the shoulder. "Yoli," he whispered. "Yoli, are you feeling okay?"

I opened my sleepy eyes, turning to his voice. It was shadowy dark in the living room where I slept, and when I turned to look at him, my whole body ached.

"I'm headed to open up the store," he explained. He'd been working there part-time since he returned from Fort Ord. "But I wanted to make sure you weren't feeling sick or dizzy or anything. Concussions can sometimes take a while before showing up."

"No, I feel fine, Chuy," I said. "I really do." His face looked pale in the dawn's gray light. He looked troubled and unsure. "Just a little sore," I added. "That's all. Really."

He sat at the foot of the couch, next to my blanketed feet. He nodded slowly, as if he were thinking of something to say but wasn't sure what. He was staring at the glass coffee table, and I turned to glance at it as well. For some silly reason the first thing I searched for was the crack in the table, even though I knew it was hidden under a crocheted doily.

"Taking you on that ride yesterday was one of the stupidest things I've ever done in my life," he said quietly.

I didn't say anything, because I was afraid that if I opened my mouth, I'd demand that he promise me that the bike ride would remain the stupidest thing he'd ever done. *Promise me that you won't do anything risky and dangerous in Vietnam. That you'll return to us.* I let these thoughts swirl in my heart with the Hail Mary, Our Father, and Hail Holy Queen prayers.

He stood up and kissed me on the forehead. "Get some sleep, Yoli bo-boli," he said.

I closed my eyes and slept.

• • •

Later in the morning when I woke up, I could hear Mamá in the kitchen opening the refrigerator door, then closing it. The sound of a pot on the stove reminded me that we were probably having our usual oatmeal with milk, raisins, and cinnamon.

When I walked into the kitchen, Mamá observed me as I sat down at the table and took my first spoonful of the lumpy oatmeal.

"This is delicious," I said, hoping to distract her from her scrutiny.

She didn't say anything as she filled two more bowls for Luz and Monica, who were still in the bathroom washing up.

"Do you have any chores for me today?" I asked her, though my sore body was hoping she'd say no.

She placed the other bowls on the table, and then sat down at the table.

"Yoli," she said. "I know you have a special bond with Chuy. And it makes me happy to know that all of you children love one another so much and protect one another so fiercely."

I stared at the lumps in the bowl.

"This is a hard time for all of us, mi'ja." Her voice caught. "We have to pray extra hard," she said. "That's all we have. We must trust that God knows best."

I quickly looked up at her. *That's all we have?* Suddenly, what I was feeling was not grief or sorrow. It was anger. It rose in me in an unexpected jolt. I opened my mouth to say something sarcastic, but I couldn't do that to Mamá. I loved her too much to disrespect her.

"These are the gift of trials," she continued.

I nodded without looking at her. Was today a good time to tell her, the day before Easter? Wouldn't it ruin that most holy day for her? And when I told her, would she stop talking to me for a week like her papi had? How disappointed she would be. I remembered Tía's words, how some mothers want a doctor or a lawyer in the family, but Mamá would love a nun or priest.

"Mamá?" I said, setting my spoon down on my half-eaten oatmeal. "I don't think I want to be a nun when I grow up." My voice was a little shaky. A little sad.

She looked at me for what seemed like a long time. "Mi'ja," she finally said, shaking her head. She was actually smiling. "You are still so young, and you have so many years yet to make a decision on what you want to do when you grow up—"

"But I know you wanted—"

"Yes, yes." She nodded, still smiling. "And my father wanted *me* to be a nun. And here I am, married with nine wonderful children."

"So, you're not disappointed in me?" I asked. "You're not mad?"

"No, mi amor." And she got up and gave me a great big hug.

THIRTY-FIVE

Easter Sunday. Yellow polyester blouses and pleated skirts for Monica, Luz, and me. I had hoped, as I watched Mamá hunched over her sewing machine these past months, she would've made me a dress to match my older sisters'. I was in junior high, after all. But when I reminded her of this—my soon-to-be señorita status—she'd looked up from the sewing machine long enough to remind *me* that the fabric was on sale "for almost nothing." Case closed, she'd positioned the presser plate and navigated down the road of perfect seams.

The only matching apparel for all five of us were wrist-length white gloves and white straw hats. Good thing I was wearing a long-sleeved blouse to hide my bandaged elbow while the gloves hid my hand scrapes. I had applied a dab of foundation to the small cut near my mouth. It would've been nice to match my older sisters, but I consoled myself by noting that my younger sisters didn't have a First Holy Communion missal yet. At least I had that over them.

But today Benjamín was not one of the altar boys. And just when I thought this would be a boring hour, I heard noisy and recognizable shuffling and guffaws. I caught a quick glimpse of the Sandoval brothers—Benjamín included!—entering the church.

Hallelujah!

They sat a couple of pews behind us, and throughout Mass I made sure to have extra-straight posture, to kneel and stand and sit slowly so my straw hat wouldn't slip off my head. And when we knelt for the closing blessing, I pressed my hands together over my mouth as if in solemn prayer. I breathed out a puff of air, checking for bad breath. Should I pop a stick of spearmint gum in my mouth before we headed out of church in case I had a chance to talk with Benjamín?

"Happy Easter!" one parishioner called out to us.

"Yes, and to you as well."

"Felices Pascuas."

"Que Dios te bendiga."

I was happy to note that our parents, along with Tía Matilde, stuck around after Mass instead of charging out of church and to our car as usual. While everyone greeted one another, I glanced this way and that, trying to not look too obvious yet hoping I might catch sight of the Sandoval family. The Easter crowd made it hard to take inventory. What I did notice was that many of the Guadalupana members came up to my mother, and I watched as she nodded slowly, somberly, while considering the words of her fellow parishioners. Were they consoling her on Chuy's impending departure, or were they commiserating? Did they have sons going off to Vietnam, too?

"Hey, Yoli, happy Easter!"

I turned to see Benjamín standing next to me. He was dressed in a navy-blue suit and a light blue paisley tie. If ever there was a moment for swooning, that was it.

"Happy Easter to you," I said. "Not an altar boy today?"

"Nope," he said. "I told Father Stadler I wanted to be sitting in the pews with my family on Easter Sunday."

"That's nice of you," I said.

"And not exactly truthful," he said, smiling.

I looked at him.

"I was afraid I wouldn't get a chance to say hi to you today, that your family would leave right away."

Was I as red as he?

"I wanted to wish you a happy Easter and tell you that I'm going to pray for Chuy, too."

I didn't say anything. My family was starting to head in the direction of the parking lot. Probably time for me to skedaddle, but I didn't want to.

I thought if I could stop time in the Saint Charles courtyard and freeze this moment with Benjamín, nothing ugly would happen. I wouldn't have to worry about Chuy returning safe, because he wouldn't be going. We'd live in this moment forever, avoiding the uncertain terrain of canyons and jungles and rivers of the future. True, I wouldn't grow up and become whatever I might've become, because I'd stay here at twelve years of age, loving my family and friends just like this. Like a twelve-year-old.

"Hey, Yoli," Ana called out to me. "Let's go."

I waved to let her know I'd heard her, be there in a minute. She trotted off to catch up with the rest.

Then turning to Benjamín, I said, "I really appreciate that. I do. Thank you. But I've got to go now." I looked toward the parking lot, which was partially obscured from view. My family was somewhere around the corner.

Then, outrageous of me (or not), I reached over and gave Benjamín a quick kiss on the cheek.

"Wow," he said, smiling hugely and probably as shocked as I was by my action. "This is my lucky day!"

I dashed away, waving to him as I caught up to my family. And I didn't care if anyone had noticed. I could barely breathe. I kissed him! I'd really, really kissed him! Instead of feeling guilty, I felt like skipping and twirling and singing at the top of a mountain. Surely God would understand. It was Easter, after all, and I needed to feel happy about something.

• • •

Lydia had a whole bunch of pesky cousins over and was babysitting them. She'd meet me at our tree after they left. "By four o'clock, these monsters better be gone, or I'll go on strike," she promised me.

I got to the tree half an hour early. This wasn't going to be easy, but I had to do it now. I was tired of carrying this inside me. Sitting in the tree alone, I figured I had to prepare myself for her not wanting to be friends anymore, and that I'd be coming to this tree alone from now on. I knew this was going to disappoint her that much. No more friendship, no more nothing.

"Yoliiiii," she called out to me. "Yodl-oh-ooh-dee." She giggled. "Yodl-ay-ee-dee."

"What's *that* all about?" I called down to her. "Your lame attempt at yodeling?"

"Yup," she said as she reached the top of the tree.

She was carrying her Easter basket filled with candy. I had mine with me as well so that we could do some trading. I looked at my loot, suddenly realizing I wasn't interested in the buttercream eggs or the colorful jellybeans, which I usually gobbled down in a handful. Even the yellow Peeps looked squished and undernourished.

"I just had an idea," she said. She was sitting on the plywood next to me. "We should go to Austria and tour the von Trapp family house. Then we can head to Switzerland, learn how to yodel, and maybe meet the *real* von Trapp family."

"I don't think they ever went to Switzerland," I said. "Carolina said so. She said it didn't happen exactly like in the movie."

"Oh," she said. "Are you sure?"

I shook my head. These days I wasn't sure about too much. Maybe it was silly of me to compare my family to the von Trapps. To whatever kind of happy ending they might have had.

"So what, Yoli! Who the heck cares?" Lydia said. "Before we join the convent, we should do something big. And since I know you love the movie, maybe there's a *Sound of Music* tour in Austria or something. And while we're there, we can visit all the cathedrals and abbeys. Kind of like a pilgrimage."

I didn't say anything.

"Maybe somewhere along the line, we'll meet the *real* Maria von Trapp and have her teach us some songs, and then we can teach our fellow nuns. I know you said you want to do your missionary work in Vietnam, but if we start a singing group, you might want to stay in the States awhile, help us out. Lead us. Especially when we're cooped up in the convent during long, cold Pennsylvania winters. We're going to need something fun to distract us so we don't get—"

"Lydia—" I began.

"—moody and depressed during the long, cold nights, and then we can start a choir like the von Trapp family and compete all over the country. The Singing Nuns Choir, we'll be called—"

"Lydia, stop—" And then I started to cry.

She didn't say anything. She glanced at me, and then at the tree, as if she'd just noticed she was sitting in one.

She reached for a small branch and began plucking the peppercorns off the twig. "Was it *The Sound of Music* or the pilgrimage idea?"

I knew she was trying to be funny, trying to cheer me up (Lydia knew me too well), but nothing seemed funny these days. And no amount of chocolate Easter eggs was going to change that; no plans to visit the von Trapps could make me feel like a winner. I felt empty and sad.

"You don't want to be a nun anymore, do you?" Like the beads of a rosary, one pink pellet after another dropped to the ground below us.

"No, I don't," I said in a croaky voice.

"I could tell," she said. "Lately, when I'd bring it up, you always wanted to change the subject. Plus, this whole friendship or whatever you have with Benjamín—"

"I'm sorry, Lydia," I said.

"You don't have to apologize, Yoli," she said. Lydia's eyes filled with tears. "I got to figuring maybe it was a dumb idea for us to be planning our lives so young. We were just eight years old when we promised each other. And hey, who knows? I might change my mind, too."

"You don't hate me?" I asked.

"Hate you?" she said. "Nah, how can I hate my best friend? You might drive me crazy with your simbolismo and your head-in-the-clouds thinking, but no, I don't hate you, Yoli. Besides, when I grow up, maybe I'll end up getting married and having a whole bunch of kids like your family."

How high could I fly?

• • •

That Easter evening, for Miss Toscano's and Chuy's and my whole family's sake—and mine, too—I wrote something positive in my diary: *April 14, 1968. Happy Easter! And oh, what an Easter it's been! A kiss on the cheek for my favorite altar boy and a heart-to-heart talk with Lydia. I don't want to be a nun anymore, Dear Diary, but I still love God and prayer and my best friend and all my family. And the von Trapps.*

THIRTY-SIX

It was like a send-off party for Chuy three weeks later, with everyone gathered on the street to wish him well. *Go with God. God protect and keep you safe. A Dios. To God I commend thee. Bless us, O Lord, and these Thy gifts. The gift of trials.*

Tía Matilde stood next to Socorrito, who had her arm locked through Don Epifranio's, his cane keeping them both upright. "Our soldier boy," the viejito whispered while Socorrito sighed and sighed again, shaking her head. El Chango, shifting on his feet, stood next to Tony and Octavio, while my four sisters made an unintentional line from oldest to youngest. Lydia and I were seated on our bikes, leaning against the fence, which was woven with sweet pea flowers. The vines meandered and coiled every which way through the slatted fencing. Unruly blossoms.

Mamá and Papá came out of the house, then Chuy and Donna, holding hands. He was dressed in his green uniform, looking, yes, like a soldier boy.

I'd promised myself I wouldn't cry. If Chuy could be brave, so could I. And besides, what good were my stupid tears going to do him? He was going to war, and that was that.

The plan was for Mamá and Papá to take Chuy to the airport, with Donna coming along. But last night as we got ready for bed, Carolina thought of a little surprise: after the four left in the Rambler, the rest of us brothers and sisters would jump into the back of El Chango's truck and surprise them by showing up at the airport. "For a grand, proper send-off," she'd whispered to us.

Hugs and kisses. Another *Go with God* and *Que Dios te bendiga*. It was noon and the blue sky was too clear, the light too bright.

After Chuy hugged and kissed everyone, I got off my bike, tapped the kickstand into place, and went to him.

He grinned at me, the silly, goofy clownish grin he'd always reserved for me when I was a little girl on the verge of crying. It always brought me to reluctant giggles. Back then, but not now.

"Study hard, Yoli bo-boli," he said as he leaned in to hug me.

I wrapped my thin arms around his waist, my head barely reaching his chest.

"And always, always," he whispered, "feel the freedom."

But I didn't let go. I closed my eyes tightly, not wanting even a little bit of the brilliant May morning to touch me. If I held on a little longer, couldn't this all go away—the draft, the war, the fear?

"We have to go now," Papá said.

Chuy kissed the top of my head and then pulled away.

Papá climbed behind the wheel while Mamá sank into the passenger seat. Chuy and Donna slipped into the back. I hopped on my bike, and as the car rolled slowly down Conifer Street, I pedaled along next to it, waving and trying on a brave smile. Just before they turned right on Hollister and picked up speed to Palm Avenue toward the freeway ramp, Chuy turned to me one last time. His playful grin, his blue eyes true and kind. He gave me a polished, clipped salute, and a wink. Then they were gone.

I skidded to a halt. I took long gulps, still trying not to cry.

Just as Lydia pulled up alongside me, I took off again and pedaled away as if my life depended on it. I pedaled so hard I thought my legs were going to fall off. When I reached the chain-link fence at the end of the street, I jumped off the bike and shoved it to the ground as if it were some piece of junk getting in my way. I started kicking the sissy basket attached to the handlebars. It cracked and crunched under my foot jabs.

"Hey, Yoli," Lydia called out, breathless, as she caught up with me. "I know you're real sad about Chuy. We all are, Yoli, but we've got to hope that he's going to be all right."

I looked at her, angry. Then I kicked the tires in the hopes of flattening them—first the front one, then the back one. Stupid bike! What was the use of feeling the freedom if you were just going to have to fight in a stupid war?

"Yoli, what are you doing?" Lydia said, her voice quivering as if she were about to start crying. "Yoli, please."

I looked at her with a rage I'd never felt before. What a crybaby! I wanted to kick her, too. I wanted her to hurt so bad she'd know what it felt like. This kind of pain. This kind of fear. I started to charge her as she stood straddled on her bike. She had a stupid little bell on her handlebar, and I wanted to rip it off. So childish, you tonta!

As I stormed toward her, I saw her eyes widen with terror, her lips part, her head pull back—and then my sobs caught in my throat. No, no, everything was ridiculously wrong! Just as I reached her, I took off running past her in a sprint, like the hundred-yard-dash champion that I was. I could see my canyon in the distance, the swath of yellow flowers and green shrubs.

"Yoli, wait!" Lydia called out again.

I was running so hard even my breath couldn't catch up with me. Almost there. And I blamed all of them—all of *us*—for not stopping Chuy from going, for not driving him to Tijuana and putting him on the next bus headed to El Grullo. To safety.

I wiped the tears from my cheeks and the snot from my nose. I was out of breath and feeling dizzy as I reached my canyon. Amid the sloshy mud and the new-growth brambles, I slipped down the embankment. Once I reached the three rickety wooden steps, I closed my eyes, certain that my favorite spot would lead me to that other world.

• • •

We're in the meadow, traipsing through the alpine countryside, where yellow sour grass blossoms have sprouted, carpeting the earth. Sparrows and goldfinches, along with the cooing of mourning doves, compete for our attention. We're headed to the other side, to the Swiss border, to freedom and safety from what Miss Toscano and everyone else I love has called a horrible war. But we're together, the nine of us kids, with Mamá leading, Tía Matilde in the middle, and Papá at the rear.

Just a little bit farther, Armando calls to me as I trail behind. He's carrying Luz piggyback. Carolina is lugging a stack of psychology textbooks.

Trudge, trudge—up, up—almost over the mountains and to the border.

We come to the culvert under the freeway. Cars and trucks and motorcycles careen overhead.

In the springtime breeze, a song: Was someone asking me to go to Scarborough Fair? Are there whispers of generals asking their soldiers to kill?

The culvert, with the stench of putrid, stagnant water, smells nothing like the meadows of the Alps. But if I belt out lively, happy songs, I can brush the bad stuff away, sing for another kind of world.

I stop a moment and watch as my family continues their march. "The Sound of Music" is playing in my mind. Or am I singing out loud?

Armando, Octavio, Chuy, Tony, Carolina, Ana, Monica, Luz, Tía Matilde, and Mamá and Papá pause and turn to look at me.

What did you say, Yoli?

I chuckle.

They can tell I'm being silly, so they smile, shake their heads, and walk on. I follow.

We're halfway across the field. Almost safe.

Soon "My Favorite Things" parades in with images not only of the von Trapps' favorite things but also of my own.

A black crow—or is it a red-tailed hawk?—glides above us. I squint. The springtime sun is in my eyes.

I continue to sing about copper kettles and woolen mittens, and soon my brothers and sisters are singing with me in perfect harmony. Our voices echo throughout the mountain range and the green alpine valley. Oh, yes, we can do this together—always together!—and then we won't feel so sad.

And when we finish singing, we hear—what is that?—a clap of thunder on this cloudless May morning.

No, not at all!

It's the Salzburg Folk Festival audience on its feet—with resounding applause—in awe of our perfectly orchestrated canticle, begging for an encore. It's plain to see that the judges favor us over the rest of the contestants, and that we're going to win.

We smile and take a bow, blow gentle kisses to our audience amid our streaming, grateful tears as they continue to applaud and chant, "Encore! Encore!" We sisters glance at one another, and then at our brothers, in relief and exhilaration. Mamá and Papá stand to the side, smiling at us. Pride and love in their eyes. We never thought we'd win, but here we are, being lauded and celebrated and told we are the winners, as if all we had to do from the beginning of our story was to sing our song.

Traipsing down the canyon and through the field, I wonder, *Who would've thought we'd triumph?* But it is so. Soon we'll hear the Benedictine monks chanting and the church bells ringing—a reminder that freedom and safety, plus a cozy Swiss fireplace and delicious apfelstrudel will be waiting for my family and me.

Thank you! Danke! ¡Gracias! We bow and bow again, with nervous giggles and grins. Smiles of utter disbelief.

• • •

Then I heard her, Lydia, calling out to me: "Yoli, come on! Everyone's ready to go to the airport."

She was at the top of the canyon, waving and motioning for me to come back. Back to her and my family. Back to Conifer Street and all my favorite things.

"Come on!" she shouted. "Please."

I paused, scanning one more time my private Alps. And I was certain—as certain as anyone could be—that there'd be other chances for folk festival wins. That no matter what the future had in store for me and my family, so long as we held one another close we'd be okay.

I stood up and waved to her. "Ya voy, ya voy," I called back to my best friend. "Jeez, I'm coming already!"

ACKNOWLEDGMENTS

I am deeply grateful to my agent, Steven Chudney, and to my exquisite editor, Margaret Ferguson, along with Janet Renard, and the entire staff at Holiday House.

My first readers—godparents to this novel—offered invaluable comments: San Diego Writers' Ink leader Tammy Greenwood, along with Will Connell, Amy Wallen, Christopher Penny, Ruth Roberts, Carol Pope, and Geoffrey Thompson. As well, Jack Madowitz, Naomi McLean, Francisco Stork, David Ulin, Hilary Schaper, Kari Wergeland, Beth Hadas, Patti Kingston, and Cathy Tkach weighed in with thoughtful observations.

Many other friends cheered me on, including Karen Johnson & Henry Krous, Kevin McLean, Roberta Balstad & Greg Withee, Mark & Karen Hughes, Birte Wise, Donna Dinan, and Locke Epsten.

I am grateful to Judy Epstein for turning on the lights when things felt dark.

I am so happy to be a part of the Madowitz connection: Mike & Larissa, Jen & Justin, Courtney & Jake, Karen & Richard, Noah, and Rachel. I am also grateful to the late Dorothy & Dr. Leon Madowitz for sharing their life stories with me.

To all my sobrinas y sobrinos, and grand- and great-grandnieces and nephews: May you remain "Primos Forever."

My utter delight and gratitude to these corazoncitos for inviting me into their world of wonder, curiosity, and imagination: Bianca, Eliseo, Gidget, Roxie, Jojo, Julian, Stella, and Judy Violet.

I salute my loving brothers and sisters: Victor, Oscar, Jorge, Gloria & Henry, Delia & Richard, Irma & Vic, and Beatriz & Héctor. And I salute the memory of my brother Sergio, who forever lives in our hearts and stories.

To the memory of Mamá and Papá, who left a wonderful legacy of love and unity.

What a gift it is for me to be the proud mother and suegra to Jessie & Isaac Béjar and Deborah & Scott Suchman. Witty, charming, and wise—there's no end to the talents of these four.

And finally, to Jack Madowitz, my cheerleader extraordinaire. You keep me sane and on track with your humor and devotion. Thank you, my love.